SAVOR the MOMENT

DANA PICCOLI

BELLA
BOOKS
2019

Bella Books, Inc.
P.O. Box 10543
Tallahassee, FL 32302

Printed in the United States of America on acid-free paper.

First Bella Books Edition 2019

Editor: Ann Roberts
Cover Designer: Judith Fellows and Dana Piccoli

ISBN: 978-1-64247-042-0

About the Author

Dana Piccoli is an entertainment writer and pop culture critic. She's the Managing Editor of the Blog at Bella Books, and has written for sites The Mary Sue, The Portalist, Screener TV, and more. She's also an experienced podcaster, moderator and event host. Dana was one of *Curve Magazine*'s Power List in Media in 2017. You can find her hanging out on Twitter talking about all things queer entertainment related @danapiccoli. She lives in South Carolina with her lovely wife and fur babies.

Acknowledgments

My first book! It's hard to believe it's even real. This romance has been in the works for over five years, and it all started with a long, boring car ride to Michigan, which gave me time to dream up this love story between Nat and Maddy.

This book would not have been possible without the support and encouragement of Linda and Jessica Hill. Thank you so much for believing in me.

A huge thank you to Ann Roberts, my editor, who has taught me so much. Your kindness and wisdom have been invaluable.

To my mother, who always told me one day I'd be a writer. I may have taken the long way around but I'm here. Thank you for your endless encouragement and always pushing me to follow my dreams, no matter how big or small.

To my father. We may not always speak the same language, but your love and support for me has never been in doubt. Thank you for putting me first your whole life.

Chelsea, Rebekah, and Kat. You three have been my greatest cheerleaders and I'm so grateful to you. You are the best mates a girl could ask for.

Lara, you and I have been on the same road for years and boy am I glad. Watching you publish your first novel was a hugely proud moment for me. Thank you for your kind words and friendship over the years.

Janice, you are the first writer I ever knew and you set one hell of an example for me. Thank you for everything.

Ryder and Evan, your input was so important to me. You are two incredible humans.

Natasha, our friendship has been a real gift and your dedication and indomitable spirit always inspire me.

And finally, to Lana, you have spent over a decade doing your best to help me achieve my dreams. I know it hasn't always been easy, but you never gave up. I love you more than anything in this world.

For Lana, with you all things are possible.

CHAPTER ONE

Nat Chambers pushed open the backstage doors with a smile. Show nights always brought out the best in her and why shouldn't she be happy? She was in a good band, no, a great band, with her best friends and was lucky enough to fall for her tour mate, Melissa Hartford. Both rising stars on the indie music scene, Nat and Melissa were a match made in musician heaven. Tonight, they would get to sing together in front of another sold-out audience and go back to their hotel together and celebrate six months of being a couple. Nat had already ordered Melissa's favorites, champagne and chocolate, from room service. Things felt like they might be getting serious and Nat wanted to make sure everything was perfect. Melissa was a real catch. Beautiful, with dark hair and piercing blue eyes, an incredible voice and a biting sense of humor. Nat pulled out her phone to see if Melissa had returned her text from earlier and was disappointed to not see a new message. Nat shrugged it off. She was probably exploring with her band and lost track of time. She was a real artist and could easily get lost in her passions.

Nat nodded to the backstage crew and headed toward her best friend and bassist Lara Bianchi's dressing room. Her other bandmate, Paul Lim, had stopped for a quick bite and a pack of cigarettes, so he'd probably be gliding in five minutes before showtime. Lara had been distant the last few days and Nat wanted to check in with her bestie and make sure she was all right. Lara had broken up with her long-time girlfriend a couple months prior and was having a rough time with it. Nat, who always wanted to be the kind of best friend you can count on, was worried Lara had fallen into a funk. Nat had been spending a lot of time with Melissa lately and made a promise to herself to make more time for Lara and Paul too. After all, without Paul and Lara's support, Nat would still be playing open mics in Brooklyn for tips and free beer.

When Nat reached Lara's dressing room, the door was closed but the lights were on, so Nat knew she'd be there. The trio had no secrets and being on tour together for so long created an open-door environment between them, so Nat found it a little odd that Lara's door was mostly closed. Nat lightly knocked on the door before pushing it open.

"Hey girl," Nat said as she let herself in. "I wanted to check in on you…" Lara was there, sitting on her dressing table with her breasts exposed and her skirt hiked up. Her blond head was thrown back in pleasure. Another woman's head was deep between her thighs, and Lara looked like she had about reached her bliss. Nat was mortified, but it's not like she'd never encountered one of her bandmates in a delicate position before.

"I am so sorry, Lara," Nat winced as she covered her eyes. "I didn't know you had someone in here. Carry on, I will see myself out." Nat started to back out of the doorway when Lara spoke, her voice full of alarm.

"Nat, oh god, no. I… I am so sorry," Lara said, her voice breaking and on the verge of tears.

Nat removed the hand shielding her eye and watched her friend of over a decade quickly cover herself as a familiar face emerged from between her legs. Melissa. Lara was a mess of blubbering tears and trembling fingers as she tried to button up her blouse and pull down her skirt. Melissa didn't speak but her face was flushed and her expression unreadable.

Nat felt vomit rise in her throat as her legs went to jelly beneath her. She grabbed the door frame to steady herself. Lara ran to her and took Nat's shoulders in her hands. Nat could feel Lara shaking her, and recognized the words coming out of her mouth, but it was like Nat was underwater and sinking fast.

"Why?" Nat managed to squeak out.

Lara dropped to her knees and wept, and it was Melissa who stepped forward. "Nat, it just happened," Melissa said, her voice flat and emotionless compared to the sobbing pile that was Lara. "Please don't make a big deal out of it, okay?"

"My best fucking friend?" she spit out like nails.

"Honey, you know I love you. This was just... It didn't mean anything."

Nat looked over to Lara who choked on her tears, her face red and puffy. She looked so ashamed that Nat had to turn away because she started to feel sorry for her.

"When?" Nat asked.

"When, what?" Melissa replied.

"When did this start?"

Melissa bit her lip, and it was Lara whose broken voice rose just barely loud enough to hear. "A month ago."

Nat let out a harsh little laugh and quickly wiped away a tear as it trickled down her face. "A month. A fucking month?"

"Lara, you should really learn to keep your mouth shut," snapped Melissa. She stepped closer to Nat until there was little space between them. "You know me. I'm just not good with being tied down. I want to for you, though. It's just...hard." Melissa ran her fingers along Nat's shoulder and Nat yanked her arm away. Melissa sighed. "Be the bigger person, Natalia. This doesn't have to change anything."

Nat swallowed and steadied herself. "Oh Melissa, this changes everything."

CHAPTER TWO

Eight Months Later…

"Okay, on the count of three. One, two, three!" exclaimed Nat as she and Paul hauled a Marshall Stack amplifier out of the van.

"Sweet Jesus," Paul panted as he pushed the amp to the side. "You know, Nat, we really need to get a new roadie."

Nat wiped a bead of sweat from her forehead. "Well, considering you slept with our last roadie and he ran out of the Denny's in St. Louis crying, I'm thinking perhaps you should hush and start working on those rippling biceps of yours."

Paul smirked and Nat couldn't help but laugh. "Nat, just because you have a strict 'no groupie or crew' policy yourself, doesn't mean the rest of us don't like to have a little fun now and then." He grabbed his kick drum and hoisted it high on his chest with a grunt. "I love you, babe, but sometimes you could stand to loosen up. You are a rock star, for chrissakes."

"I'm not a rock star," she said with mock indignation, her shoulders held back "I'm a moderately successful singer/ songwriter." He rolled his eyes with a smile as she picked up a Zildjian cymbal from the floor of the van and spun it on her finger. "And see? I've got mad skills. This is what I do when you and Jackie are off partying and getting laid." The cymbal made a whooshing sound as it circled her finger.

"Very nice. The ladies will be very impressed. By the way, where is Jackie?" He put down the drum and scanned the backstage area. "We could use a little help!"

"I'll check the sound booth. She's probably offering her unsolicited advice to a very receptive soundman." Nat shielded her eyes from the stage lights and peered out into the house. "Jackie, can you get your cute lil' self up here and help Paul and me unload the rest of the van?"

"Coming, darlings!" called a lyrical British accent from the top of the house. "Tell Paul to quit his whining." With that Nat's other bandmate Jackie Adeyemi came bounding down the aisle, her dark ponytail swinging with every step. When she reached the stage, Nat hoisted her up.

"I can already tell the acoustics in here are choice," Jackie said as she gave Nat a quick pat on the cheek. She blew a giant kiss to the sound guy, while secretly giving him a finger only Nat could see. Nat laughed as Jackie skipped off to help Paul and smacked him on the ass when she got there. Nat could hear them in the distance.

"Look there, you don't even need me! Bob's your uncle!" teased Jackie in her exaggerated British accent.

Paul picked up the petite cello player in a bear hug. "God, I love you, but I can't understand a damn thing you say." He put her down before they disappeared onto the loading dock.

Nat smiled to herself; how she adored her band, this life. The stage beneath her feet was well worn and solid. It felt like it held the notes of a million songs that played before her. Tonight was the last night of the final leg of their US tour and tomorrow the Nat Chambers Band would head home to NYC for some well-deserved rest before they started work on their new album. Life was perfect. Well, maybe not perfect, but close enough.

CHAPTER THREE

Nat slid the key into the door of her Long Island City loft and breathed an exhausted sigh of relief. Life on the road, while exciting, was nothing compared to her nice warm bed and coffee in her own kitchen. When she opened the door, there stood her main man, Eddie. She bent down to rub his furry gray head, and he chirped and purred a welcome home. She brought in her guitar and suitcase as Eddie made figure eights between her feet. She made her way into the living room, where there was a note from Oliver Vargas, her full-time manager and part-time cat sitter.

Welcome home, beautiful. Hope the last show went off without a hitch. Take a few days to regroup, then give me a call. Lots to talk about, good things.

Oliver.

Ps...there is your favorite Thai takeout waiting for you in the fridge.

Pps. Your cat is an asshole.

Nat snorted a laugh and looked at Eddie, who now lounged on the couch and licked his nether regions. "Classy. What did you do this time, buddy?" Eddie washed his face and avoided the question. Nat opened the fridge, which was empty except for a bottle of Sauvignon Blanc and a container of Pad Thai.

"Sweet ambrosia! Oliver, you are a goddamn saint, you know that?" She'd thank him in person soon enough, but now it was time to become one with the wine and noodles. She poured herself a glass and took a long sip. It was so beautifully grassy and herbaceous; she nearly teared up with joy. She took the glass and the Pad Thai and plopped herself on the couch next to Eddie. Grabbing the remote she channel surfed and stopped when she heard her own voice singing back at her. As the opening credits of the popular med school drama *Trauma University* rolled, so did her song, which had been chosen as the show's familiar theme music.

Three years earlier, her song "Heart/Break" was chosen to play in the opening title sequence of the new show. Little did she know it would go on to be such a huge hit and gain her legions of new fans, not to mention boost her record sales. (It also scored her a make-out session with one of the shows gorgeous female leads in a bathroom stall at the show's premiere party.) After years of struggling to make rent and cover touring expenses, The Nat Chambers Band now sold out shows in college towns and bigger cities alike. She was able to buy her loft outright, pay off all her credit cards and live comfortably for the first time in her adult life.

She raised her glass to the screen. "Cheers, you beautiful bastards."

Her phone chirped signaling a text message. She looked at Eddie, who was twisted into a ball, with just one eye open. Thinking it was Paul or Jackie checking in, she grabbed the phone. However, she immediately regretted reading the message. It wasn't from her bandmates. In fact, it was the one person she decidedly did not want to hear from. Melissa.

Hi Natalia. Heard your tour was a success. Welcome home.

She tossed the phone across the room where it landed with a thud against the love seat. She drank the rest of her wine in a big gulp, turned off the TV, and marched to her bedroom, leaving her noodles uneaten on the coffee table. Eddie gave them a sniff and then followed his owner into the dark hallway toward the bedroom. She peeled off her jeans and undid her bra, leaving them haphazardly on the floor. She dove face first into the mattress and waited a moment before she released a long and muffled, "Fuuuuuuuuucck."

CHAPTER FOUR

"And now let's move into Sun Salutation," the yoga instructor said softly as she canvassed the room. Nat, Paul, and Jackie had made a pact to get in shape and decompress after the tour. Hot yoga classes at The Space in Park Slope were on the agenda. The instructor, an attractive older woman with a gray pixie cut, passed by and corrected Nat's posture. Paul and Jackie were on either side of her and Jackie was simultaneously texting and posing, while beads of sweat poured off Paul's red face. It had been a few days since the trio arrived back in New York, and Nat was doing her best to avoid Melissa's texts and drinking a bit more wine than she should. Her muscles were tight and dehydrated, and she felt a little unsteady on her feet, but she needed this release.

"Natalia, I'm dying. I'm actually dying," whimpered Paul, the nicotine leaching out in his sweat.

"You're not dying. You smoke two packs a day and you are a handsome, husky fool."

"Didn't you hear? I'm vaping now."

"Focus please, ladies and gentlemen," announced the instructor. Nat's face grew red with embarrassment. "Let's move into Downward Dog."

Nat pulled herself into the inverted V position, and while holding the pose, she looked toward the floor to ceiling windows. Right beyond Jackie, who was somehow taking a selfie, Nat noticed a woman with wavy red hair. She had toned arms the color of fresh cream dotted with light, playful freckles. Her shoulders were bare and defined, glistening with perspiration, leading into a raspberry colored tank top. Just as Nat was thinking how lovely it would be to run her fingertips across those beautiful arms, the woman turned her head and met Nat's gaze. Her lips curled into a grin that took Nat by surprise, so much so, that her sweaty hands gave way underneath, sending her tumbling from her pose, her head smacking against the blond wood floor of the studio. Everything went black.

When Nat opened her eyes, Jackie and the instructor knelt above her. She felt a knot rising on her forehead as Jackie applied a cold ice pack. Paul appeared with a cup of water, his face still red.

"You'll be just fine," said the instructor. "I'm a former nurse, and I don't think you have a concussion. Just a small bump. Might be wise to get it checked out by your general practitioner, though. Can you stand?" Nat nodded and Jackie and Paul helped her up. She was a little sore but more embarrassed than anything. Her first thought was what an ass she had made of herself in front of that beautiful stranger. The rest of class had cleared out during the hubbub, so Nat, Jackie, and Paul gathered their mats and belongings as well. As they headed toward the lobby, the beautiful redhead rose from the window seat.

"Is she okay?" she asked Paul. She turned her concerned gaze toward Nat. "Are you okay?" Nat, touched that the redhead had waited to check on her prognosis, smiled and nodded yes. The redhead smiled back. Nat opened her mouth to speak, but the room was still spinning a bit, so she thought better of it.

"Oh, good." The redhead slipped her mat under her arm. "Feel better," she whispered before heading through the front door and out to the street.

Jackie poked Nat playfully in the ribs, bringing her back to reality.

"Wanna skip coffee?" Paul asked.

Nat reached up to brush some hair away from the swollen goose egg. "It's too early for bourbon, right?"

"Oh girl, it is never too early for bourbon," remarked Paul.

Jackie cocked her head at him.

"What?" he shrugged.

"Coffee is good. I could use a boost. Let's go," Nat declared as she linked arms with her friends.

CHAPTER FIVE

Nat and Jackie stirred their lattes at a café table in the coffee shop downstairs from the yoga studio. Paul stomped over with a magazine in his hand. "You are never going to believe this shit." He tossed it on the table, causing the empty sugar packets to flutter onto the floor in its wake. It was a copy of the weekly indie rock magazine *Market*, and on the cover was none other than Melissa Hartford.

"Sweet Agony Lead Singer Melissa Hartford: Uncovered," Jackie read aloud nonchalantly.

"They should hurry and cover the bitch back up," sniffed Paul as he took his seat.

Nat took a long sip of her coffee and the table was quiet for a moment.

Jackie broke the silence, her brown eyes flashing between them. "Soooo… Is anyone going to tell me the real story? I know you and Melissa had a thing and then a falling out of sorts—"

"Of sorts? Well, that's the goddamn understatement of the year," Paul said.

"All right, easy, mate," Jackie said. "But I want to know the whole story. Since I came on board this tour, I've only heard bits and pieces from Paul."

Nat shot a look at Paul, who shrugged his shoulders and said, "What? We share a van, for chrissakes. Long, lonely nights. I mean, frankly, I'm surprised I didn't spill all the damn tea."

"It's fine," Nat sighed as she shifted in her chair. She paused for a moment, then flipped the paper over. "Last year, Melissa Hartford's band and our band booked a North American multi-city double bill. That much you know." Jackie leaned forward with her hands under her chin. "Well, things were great at first. Melissa and I...hit it off."

He rolled his eyes. "More like they spent every waking moment together," he interjected, "which was annoying by the way."

"Would you like to tell the story?"

"Well, I tell it much better," he said with a smile.

"Fine," She leaned back in her chair and gestured for him to continue.

He pulled his chair closer to Jackie. "Okay, so Natalia falls head over heels for Melissa, who is a soul sucking monster with really nice boobs and bouncy hair."

"It was quite bouncy," Nat agreed as she chewed on the end of her stir straw.

"Right, so these two are all duets and love songs and guesting in each other's sets and shit. The crowds didn't know for sure, but they could feel the energy and they loved it. They called them Natlissa."

"I thought it was HartChamber?" Nat interjected.

"Whatever. The point is, they shipped it."

Jackie narrowed her eyes. "Shipped it?"

He sighed. "Yes, it's short for relationship. Are you ever on Twitter? Get with it, Jackie. Anyway..."

Paul then proceeded to tell the story of the worst day of Nat's life.

"Oh, bloody hell!" exclaimed Jackie who looked at Nat with horror. Nat ran her fingers through her hair and pursed her lips.

"It was worse than you can imagine," Paul continued. "Nat, Lara, and I still had to perform three more shows together. Nat didn't speak to anyone save for me that last week. She breezed past Melissa during and after shows. To Nat's credit, she was one hundred percent professional. Said she didn't want to punish the fans for something out of their control. Lara was all tears and apologies. She begged Nat to forgive her. I mean they were bandmates and friends for years."

"Some things you can't get past," Nat said as she peered out the café window.

"What about Melissa?" Jackie asked looking to Paul.

"Melissa was nonchalant, to say the least. She made it seem like Nat had never meant that much to her in the first place and that they were just having fun. I think that's what hurt Nat the most." Paul looked into Nat's eyes, which were welling with tears. He reached over and brushed her cheek with his thumb. "I'm sorry, love," he said gently.

"It's the head bump."

"Sure, doll." He returned his focus to Jackie. "After that, Nat let Lara go and decided to go with a fresh new set up. Bass out, cello in. That's where you came in."

Jackie smiled.

"And we're all the better for it, right Natalia?"

Nat took a deep breath. "Absofuckinglutely," she cheered as she raised her paper cup to her bandmates. Paul and Jackie joined her in the toast.

"So, speaking of that, Oliver wants us to get back in the studio soon," Nat announced. "Which would be fine if I'd been able to write any decent new songs in months."

Paul slurped his coffee. "What about that one you played for me last week? The one in six-eight?"

"It was shit. I tossed it."

"I thought it was good."

"It was trite and passionless."

He laughed. "Those are some of my best qualities."

"Well," Jackie piped in, "perhaps you need a little inspiration. You seemed pretty inspired before you went all ass over tit during yoga." She cast a raised eyebrow at Nat.

"How did you even see that? You were taking a picture of your own boobs," Nat responded.

"I'm an excellent multi-tasker. Come on, I play cello and sing harmonies at the same time. I'm goddamn spectacular!"

"That you are." Nat smiled. "Considering I literally fell flat on my face in front of her, I'm going to venture to say that I didn't make the best first impression."

"I wouldn't be too sure about that," Jackie said with a knowing smile. "Even I felt those sparks."

Nat chuckled at that thought. "Sparks, eh? No, that was the look of pity for a poor woman who is apparently as coordinated as a newborn giraffe."

"Nah, there was definitely sparkage, right Paul?" Jackie playfully punched him in the arm.

"Loads. Sparks. Sparkles. Glitter!"

Nat couldn't help but smile. Could there really have been sparks? No way.

CHAPTER SIX

Nat sat in bed, carefully licking orange cheese dust off her fingers. In the two days since she'd fallen ass over tit at the yoga studio, she'd been nursing her wounds and laying low. It wasn't so much the bump on the head, but the conversation with Paul and Jackie afterward.

Seeing Melissa on the cover of that magazine shook her. She'd spent the last year trying not to think about Melissa, and all that did was remind her of the pain and frustration of the situation. She hadn't dated anyone since the breakup, and the double whammy of losing one of her best friends along with her lover was too much to bear. She'd compartmentalized it, but sometimes she just had to admit it really sucked. So there she sat in bed, Eddie sprawled out on his back in a sunbeam, while she looked disheveled and covered in a thin layer of nacho cheese powder. She ignored a soft knock at the door and searched through Netflix for something to watch for the umpteenth time. With annoyance, she tossed her iPad and laid down in a huff.

"Chambers, you look like shit," Paul said, suddenly standing in the door frame of her bedroom.

She screamed with surprise. "Jesus H, Paul! What are you doing here and why are you trying to kill me?" She tossed a throw pillow at him.

He gingerly held up a keychain. "Remember, I have a key?"

"That's for emergencies only."

Paul shrugged and sat down on the bed. "You didn't respond to my text for like, five hours. I figured that meant emergency. But now that I see you, I'm guessing…more lezmergency than actual emergency."

She glared at him. "Lezmergency?"

"Yeah," he said as he picked up little pieces of trash and discarded clothing from the bed. "It's when your lesbian best friend is brooding over a woman and you have to come and try to fix it."

"Who says I'm brooding?"

"Well, the state of your hair for one thing. Also, I know that the Melissa thing got under your skin the other day." He pulled out a joint and offered it to her. She shook her head. "Good thinking." He lit up and took a drag. "You are the worst on pot."

"Thanks. Remind me again why you're here? Just to torture me?"

He grabbed her by the shoulders. "That's always fun but no, I'm here on official best friend business. So, let it out."

She huffed. "There's nothing to let out."

"Bullshit." He took another drag and blew it out the side of his mouth. "I can see you are hurting, so let's talk."

She pulled at a loose thread on her comforter. "Fine. I guess, it's just that every time I think it's over, that I'm not hurt or angry anymore, something happens to remind me that I'm not over it."

"Maybe it's not that you aren't over it. Maybe, it's that you hold on tightly to things, even pain, and it brings you some sort of weird comfort to have this big bad emotion in your life."

She scrunched her eyebrows. "That's nonsense."

"Is it?" He stubbed out the joint on a nearby plate of cookie crumbs. "Do you still love Melissa?"

"No," she said with assurance. She didn't.

"Do you miss her?"

"God, no."

He motioned for her to move over and he laid next to her. "So, it comes down to pride then?"

"What? No. I don't know. Maybe."

"I mean, it makes sense. If our roles had been reversed, my pride would have been wounded too. The ego is a bitch of a thing to battle against. I think, and I may be wrong, but I doubt it, that you're more hurt about Lara than Melissa."

Nat's stomach dropped at the mention of Lara's name. Friends since their early days in New York, Nat and Lara had been more like sisters than friends. "I hate to admit it, but you may have a point. I put so much anger toward the situation, I didn't really take the time to process how sad I was about it."

"Uh-huh."

"I don't miss Melissa but I do miss Lara."

He leaned on one elbow. "I wasn't going to tell you this, but now that you're having your come to Jesus moment, I think you can handle it."

"Okay?" She prepared herself for the worst.

"I ran into Lara the other day."

"Really? Where? Last I heard she was moving to LA."

"She did. She was in town for a gig, I guess. We bumped into each other in Hell's Kitchen on the street. New York is such a small town."

"Well?"

"She's good. She let her hair grow out. She's working with a new band she likes a lot. She was with a guy who it turns out is her boyfriend. Cute."

"Is this supposed to make me feel better?"

He sneered. "I'm getting there. Anyhoo, she asked about you. Told me she misses you a lot and regrets what happened every day. She's happy now but she wished she could change how things happened. Turns out Melissa told her you guys were opening up the relationship and that she didn't have to worry."

"That dick."

"Yeah, exactly. I mean, it's not like she was using that as an excuse, because let's face it, fucking your best friend's girlfriend under any circumstance is not cool."

Nat rubbed her face. "And?"

"And, she's sorry. She was also harboring this hidden jealousy of you, and it found a way to worm its way out in the worst possible way."

"She said that?"

"Yeah, she's been doing a lot of meditation and therapy. Don't roll your eyes."

"I didn't!"

"You wanted to. The point of all this is, Lara is really sorry and she wanted you to know that. I know it's not the closure you were probably looking for, but it's out there in the universe now if you want to grab hold of it."

Nat sat quietly for a moment. She wanted to forgive Lara and maybe that was the key to moving forward. "I'll think about it."

"Okay, you do that. Meanwhile, I'll order us some Chinese while you take a shower. You smell like regret and processed cheese. Normally that's appealing to me in a person, but not today, buddy." He hopped up and headed into the living room. Eddie trotted behind him, hoping for a treat.

Nat sniffed her armpits and decided Paul's advice was best taken.

CHAPTER SEVEN

Nat sat in the rehearsal studio the next day with a pen in her hand and stared at the empty page before her. Well, technically it wasn't empty. It was full of false starts and crossed out lines, so in her experience that was as good as a big, fat nothing. She sighed and tossed the pen across the room. It accidently bounced and whizzed past Jackie's ear as she rosined her bow.

"Oi!"

Nat sat up. "Oh my god, I'm sorry! I have terrible aim. I can't do sports."

"Apparently," Jackie scoffed as she resumed rosining.

"Once, when I was a kid, my parents sent me to softball camp. It was a nightmare. Not only did I hit the girl I had a crush on in the nose with a runaway pitch, but I also fell asleep in the outfield. I was subsequently shunned…and pantsed."

"I was rather good at sports," Jackie replied, blowing some light, sticky dust from her bow. "I was on the football team. It was rather like *Bend it Like Beckham*, but without all the lesbian subtext. At least for me."

"Yes, I know. You are tragically straight."

Jackie pursed her lips. "I really am. I tried in college, Nat. I really did. I just couldn't get it to take."

Nat laughed.

"Anyway, my parents were worried it would interfere with my classical studies so they pulled me out."

"And how did they take it when you left the classical world to play rock music?"

"Oh, about as well as damp squib. Imagine having to tell your Nigerian parents that you are leaving the symphony to travel the world with a bunch of American girls with blue hair and nipple piercings."

"Ah yes, your first band. How was touring with Moxie?"

Jackie rolled her eyes. "Well, it was rather like *Bend it Like Beckham*, but *with* all the lesbian subtext."

"I heard that about them."

Jackie ran her bow across the cello's D string, moving her finger and creating a beautiful vibrato. "Then somehow I ended up with you corkers."

"Thank you. I think. That's a compliment, right?"

Jackie threw her head back and laughed. "Yes, it is. Beau is itchy, Nat. He wants to play new songs. What have you got for us?"

She cocked her head. "Wait, your bow's name is Beau?"

Jackie narrowed her eyes. "Well of course it is. What kind of musician doesn't give their instrument a proper name?"

She looked over to where her guitar, Tiffany, sat in its stand. Jackie had her there.

"I'm trying here. I know there's got to be something in there," She pointed to her head. "I mean, there always has been but it's…stuck."

"You would have thought that bump to the head would have knocked something loose," Jackie said, using Beau to point at Nat's bump.

Nat shrugged. "I guess it's going to take something more than a knock on the noggin."

Jackie cleared her throat. "Maybe it's not a something but a someone you need."

"Ha, please," she laughed bitterly. "That's how I got into this mess in the first place."

Jackie sighed and dropped Beau to her side. "I'm just saying maybe it's time to allow yourself to be inspired again."

She shook her head and turned back to her music notebook. But as Jackie put Beau to work, Jackie's words spun around Nat like the notes coming from her cello.

CHAPTER EIGHT

As Nat arrived at the yoga studio the following Saturday, her phone vibrated in her pocket. She figured it was Melissa, who had texted her a dozen times, so she let it be. She turned the corner into the changing room and secretly hoped to see the cute redhead again. Finding the locker room empty, she tossed her bag to the floor with a sigh, sat down and fiddled with her mat.

"How's your head?"

The voice startled her. The redhead walked toward her from behind a set of lockers, undoing her ponytail. Nat sat wide-eyed, mouth slightly agape.

"I'm so sorry, did I scare you?" she asked, obviously embarrassed.

"Uh, oh, no… Well maybe a little," Nat admitted with a smile, which she hoped would put the redhead at ease.

"Well, I'm glad to know I'm not the only one who didn't get the message."

She offered a confused look, and the redhead lifted her phone. "The teacher had to cancel at the last minute. Looks like we're the only ones here," she said, motioning to the empty changing room. "So...your head?"

Nat touched the bump she'd sustained the week before. "Oh, this? Pshh. This is nothing. I've nearly regained my motor functions. I'm fine."

"I'm Madeline LaDuke. Maddy," she said, arm outstretched to Nat.

Nat stood and took Maddy's hand in her own.

"I'm Nat...Chambers."

Her face didn't register anything other than a warm smile. Nat was used to being recognized and she was at once relieved and disappointed.

"Well, Nat...Chambers, it looks like I've got some time to kill before my shift now that we won't be sun salutating. I don't suppose you'd like to join me for a cup of coffee?"

A flutter rose in Nat's stomach. "I think I could swing that."

"Great, lemme just grab my jacket."

She admired Maddy as she gathered her belongings. Her shoulder length red hair hung in loose, beautiful ringlets. Maddy's yoga clothes accentuated her petite frame perfectly, a V-neck T-shirt revealing a smattering of freckles on her chest.

"Okay, ready?" Maddy asked as she slung her bag over her shoulder.

Nat shot up from her seat and hoped Maddy didn't notice her staring. "Yep, awesome."

They stopped by the coffee shop downstairs ordering a latte for Nat and a hot chocolate for Maddy. There was no seating available, so Maddy suggested they take a walk.

"I absolutely love New York this time of year, don't you? Right after the snow starts to melt and the air changes. There's this kind of stillness." Maddy turned and flashed a smile at Nat, who couldn't help but notice how full and pink Maddy's lips were against the bright white of her teeth.

"Hot chocolate, I see," Nat observed. "Not a coffee person?"

"I just have a wicked sweet tooth. I guess that explains how I ended up a pastry chef."

"A pastry chef? Wow, I can't even make pancakes so you have just blown my mind." Maddy laughed at her self-deprecation. "Where do you practice this dark magic, may I ask?"

"Touché, it's on the Lower East Side."

"I know Touché. It's one of the hottest tickets in town! I do believe I read about these epic deserts of yours in the Daily Press. Didn't the reviewer give you six stars or something?"

"Five and a half, but who's counting? The bastard," Maddy said with a crooked smile.

Nat noticed a free bench and motioned to her.

"So, what do you do, Nat, dot dot dot, Chambers?"

"I'm not gonna live that down now, am I?" she asked with a sigh. "I'm a musician."

"That sounds exciting. What do you play?"

"Guitar, but I'm a vocalist when it comes down to it. I'm a perfectly mediocre guitarist, so I just sing loud enough so no one notices."

"That sounds like a genius move."

"Why, thank you," she said with exasperation. "I'm glad someone finally recognized that."

Maddy giggled and took a sip of her hot chocolate. When she looked back at Nat, she had a small peak of whipped cream on her nose. Nat bit her lip, trying not to smile.

"What?" asked Maddy, her eyes still fixed on Nat.

"Uh, well, you have a little bit of whipped cream right here." She took a napkin and gently wiped the cream from Maddy's nose. Her cheeks grew as red as her hair, but the two women's gazes remained locked. Maddy's eyes were beautiful. They weren't quite green, definitely not brown, something golden and gorgeous.

"Hazel," Nat murmured out loud, accidentally.

"I'm sorry?"

"Oh, uh nothing. I was just thinking about hazelnuts. Do you make anything with hazelnuts?" Nat blurted, hoping to save some face.

"Not at the moment, but I like to rotate the menu every week or so. Summer is the best time because everything is fresh and in season. I try to stay true to that whenever possible. In the fall, I love to go upstate and pick a ton of apples and feature those."

"That's excellent. Nothing like a New York apple."

"I know it's a cliché but it's so true," Maddy said, her natural blush looking not unlike that on a perfect apple.

"Do you live in the neighborhood?" Nat asked, hoping she didn't sound like a creep. She stopped herself from saying, "I promise not to stalk you."

Maddy shook her head. "No, I live on the Lower East Side. I just really like this studio. It's not super pretentious and the teacher is a bit of a mommi."

"Mommy?"

"Yeah, mommi with an 'I.' It's like the lesbian version of a daddy."

Nat couldn't help but laugh. "Well thank you for this education today. Come to think of it, lesbians do love them some middle-aged women."

"It's the truth. This is a conversation I was not expecting to be having today." Maddy giggled.

"Well, who's your favorite middle-aged Mommi, then?"

"Mmm, Cate Blanchett for sure. What about you?"

"I'm going to say…Viola Davis."

"Good choice."

"So besides fantasizing about older women, what do you like to do for fun?" Nat wondered if this question was too bold. Did Maddy think she was going to ask her out? *Was* she going to ask Maddy out?

Maddy took a long sip of her hot chocolate. "Honestly, I spend a lot of time at work and when I'm not there, I'm trying to come up with recipes at home. Basically, I'm a pastry nerd."

"Well, turns out, that is one of my favorite genres of Lifetime Christmas movie," she said, letting herself flirt a little.

"Oh my god, you watch those?" Maddy asked, without any sarcasm in her voice.

"Yes?" she replied, hoping it wouldn't pin her as a total cheeseball.

"I freaking love those."

She breathed a sigh of relief.

Maddy continued. "Too bad there are no gay holiday rom-coms. Can you imagine?"

"I totally could. *It Came Upon a Midnight Queer*."

Maddy guffawed. "Or how about, *Make the Yuletide Really Gay*?"

"Good one. Wait, how about, *Meet Me Under The Mistletoe, You Big Ol' Lesbian*?"

"That one is a bit on the nose, but I would totally watch it," Maddy said. "My stomach hurts from laughing."

Nat loved the way Maddy looked when she laughed. It was really beautiful and her laughter was contagious. "Me too. I can keep going if you like."

Maddy checked the time on her phone. "I would really love too but I need to get to the restaurant and start prepping for tonight's service."

"Oh sure, sure," Nat said as they rose from the bench.

"Thank you for joining me for the walk. It was really nice to talk to you. You should come down to Touché sometime. This week, it's all about huckleberries that I preserved last fall."

"Huckleberries, well, how can a girl possibly pass that up?"

"I prep during the day, but I'm usually there after six as well. I hope to see you again." Maddy reached out and placed her hand lightly on Nat's forearm and gave it a quick squeeze.

"Me too, Maddy. Have a good one." She watched her walk away, her crimson curls flowing behind her.

Nat's phone buzzed again in her pocket, interrupting the view, but seeing it was her manager, she answered. "Oliver Vargas, what do I owe the pleasure?"

"Nat, sweetness, are you feeling well rested?"

"Not too shabby. By the way, you are a god among men. That Sauvignon was divine. Eddie sends his love."

"Oh man, that damn cat is always looking at me like I'm his next meal. Listen, let's talk tomorrow about the new album. While we're on the subject, how's the writing coming along?"

She winced at the question. She'd been suffering this major bout of writer's block since ending things with Melissa. It was a claustrophobic, helpless feeling, like having one arm tied behind her back.

"Good, great. Coming along."

"That's what I love to hear. How about two? I'll take to you lunch."

"Well if lunch is involved I can certainly clear my dance card. Text me the details. I'll see you then."

As Nat slipped the phone back in her pocket, she felt guilty for not being honest with Oliver. He'd ask her more about these new songs, but hopefully, she could come up with something satisfying to tell him. She put it out of her mind for then, because the thought of Maddy in her yoga pants was far more pleasant. She lamented not getting Maddy's number. She was still buzzing from their conversation, and while it was brief, she knew she wanted to see her again—soon.

She pulled her phone back out. "Hello, this is Nat Chambers. I'd like to make a reservation, dinner for one. When's the next availability? Tomorrow at 10 is perfect. Thanks." She smiled dreamily to herself. "Huckleberries."

CHAPTER NINE

Nat paused in front of her reflection in the restaurant window and ran her hand through her hair. Hair that somehow always had the ability to look like she's just rolled out of bed, no matter how much expensive product she put in it. She sighed as her messy, dark brown bangs refused to cooperate with her fingers rugged urging. Oliver was always so put together in his fine, yet playful suits, and she was already nervous about seeing him. She debated confessing to her lack of artistic prosperity. She gave her hair one last fruitless ruffle. *Fuck it. I'm a musician.*

She pushed open to the door of the restaurant and was greeted by a young, attractive hostess with jet-black hair, red lipstick and five-inch heels. The hostess smirked and sized her up. She felt slightly out of place in her fitted black leather pants and distressed red tank top, but thankfully she'd grabbed a tailored black blazer as she headed out the door.

The hostess seemed to approve or at least recognized her, because she breathily announced, "Good afternoon, Miss Chambers. Please follow me."

She followed her through the restaurant until she saw a familiar face. Oliver stood to greet her. He looked handsome in his salmon button down and camel colored light wool pants.

"Natalia! You are only fifteen minutes late today. I'm so proud of you," he teased as he kissed her cheek.

"I know, that's like arriving early in my world."

He motioned for her to sit. The hostess placed her menu in front of her and let her hand graze her shoulder as she walked back to the stand. He raised his eyebrows at her and snorted a laugh. She shrugged her shoulders and he shook his head.

"How the hell do you do that?"

"Do what?"

"Exactly."

She rolled her eyes. The waiter came by and Oliver took the liberty of ordering for them. "A Remy VSOP and ginger and a Cobb Salad for me. The lady will have a club soda with two limes and a warm spinach salad."

"No onions," they said in unison.

He thanked the waiter. "So, let's get down to business, shall we? I've got big news."

"Big, eh? Big can be awesome, or very, very scary."

"This big is very awesome. *Trauma University* recently was picked up for distribution in the UK, Germany and France. It started airing this week and already we've seen a big boost in your online sales." He paused as the waiter delivered their drinks.

She took a long sip of her soda. "So yes, that is great news. What now?"

"Well, ideally, we get you back on tour as soon as possible, this time with a few dates in Europe."

She threw her head back. "Oooolliver. We just got back from tour. Three months on the road. We need a break. I need a break."

"I get that, I do," he said as he reached a hand across the table and placed it on hers. "But we need to strike while the iron is hot. This could mean big things for you. A whole new audience."

"When?" she asked curtly.

"Three months from now. We would kick it off with a quick domestic show in Philly for the Watershed Club's twenty-year anniversary. I know you played some of your first big shows there, so that's a given. Then off to Europe for a three-week wham, bam, thank you ma'am. Then when you get back, we will get you recording that new album. What do you say?"

"I say I hope you chip one of your veneers on that Cobb salad," she replied with exaggerated spite. "I have to talk to Paul and Jackie first."

"Already done. They're on board." The waiter placed their salads in front of them.

"Fantastic, I've lost control over my own band. Fine. Let's do this," she said, knowing full well that she didn't have much choice in the matter.

He picked up his fork and gave her a big wink. "How's the new material coming along?"

"Great. It's great. It's got a lot of potential. I think you'll like it," she lied again, this time feeling less guilty about it. "Um, can you excuse me for a moment? I need to run to the ladies' room."

He nodded and tipped his drink in her direction. She made a beeline to the bathroom and braced herself on the sink. Another tour. The travel, the bad food, the late nights. Her heart just wasn't in it. Then for some reason, her mind flashed to Maddy, whipped cream on her nose. She felt warm all over and she couldn't help but smile, knowing she'd see her later tonight at Touché.

Just as she turned the knob of the faucet, the hostess walked in. Nat smiled politely, and before she even had the chance to excuse herself, the hostess pushed her against the wall and kissed her hard on the mouth. Nat, completely taken aback, just stood frozen as the hostess slipped a piece of paper in her pocket and whispered in her ear, "I'm Selina. Text me." She walked away as quickly as she had appeared. Nat looked in the mirror, red lipstick smeared on her face. She shook her head as she wiped off the evidence of this bizarre little encounter. She reached into her pocket and took out Selina's number. She thought about the freckles on Maddy's pale shoulders and crumpled the paper and tossed it in the trash on her way out the door.

Back at the table the conversation turned to numbers and tour details. She picked at her salad, answering Oliver's questions and carefully dodging specific questions about her new material. After the check was paid and she was ready to leave, Oliver stopped her.

"One more thing, Natalia."

She glanced at him sideways. "Hmm, you only call me Natalia when I'm in trouble or you are."

He dismissively shook his head, but she was unconvinced. "This would be not until the next summer, after the Euro tour and the new album recording. After a nice long, deserved break."

"I'm listening."

"Well, I was approached by Melissa Hartford's agent and they want to give the joint tour another go…"

She tossed her napkin on the table and stood. "No longer listening."

"Just hear me out. The tour made you both a lot of money and it's a purely practical option. I know that you have issues with Melissa, but—"

"No, Oliver, you apparently don't know," she whispered angrily. "Because if you did know, if you knew me at all, you wouldn't dream of putting me in this position." With that, she turned around and walked away.

He called after her. "Nat, I'm sorry. Forget it. I'll tell them we pass."

"Damn fucking right we'll pass," she called over her shoulder before swinging open the door, avoiding eye contact with Selina on her way out.

Out on the street, her head was spinning. It's not that she wanted or missed Melissa. She just wanted to be done feeling so bad about her. She had never been betrayed like that before and the thought of it made her sick, not to mention she grieved for her decimated friendship with Lara. She clenched her fists and shoved them into her pockets. There would be no escaping Melissa Hartford. Her face would be on album covers and magazines, her songs playing over speakers at hipster department stores.

She cut through the throngs of tourists, slipping down lesser populated streets. When she was a young singer, living on dollar dumplings from Chinatown and sleeping on an air mattress, she would walk the streets of the city to clear her head—The Upper East Side, with its streets lined with brownstones and beautiful architecture. Chelsea, with its beautiful boys and ever-changing facades. Wherever her feet would take her, she would go. So, with her head pounding and her heart aching, she walked. By the time she reached the inlet to Central Park, she felt lighter. No more Melissa. She was going to leave those thoughts in Strawberry Fields. She'd go on tour like Oliver and the label wanted, and she'd make a new record. But first, she was going to find herself some inspiration, and she had a good idea where to start.

CHAPTER TEN

Touché was buzzing that night. Nat could feel the energy when she walked in the door. People laughed and music flowed soft and seamless. She scanned the restaurant and found it had an open kitchen. She had planned to send a note back to Maddy about her certain-to-be-a-lovely meal, but it turned out to be unnecessary. Maddy was standing right behind a chef's island, surrounded by seating, preparing desserts for the entire world to see. The host checked Nat's name off the reservation list and led her to a table near the back of the restaurant. She gently touched his arm.

"Excuse me, I don't suppose there's an available seat near the kitchen?" She motioned to where Maddy was standing.

"Certainly, Miss. Follow me."

Maddy was absorbed in a very delicate plating of dessert as Nat saddled up to the island. Maddy carefully garnished the plate and presented it to a waiter, her red hair in a side braid and held back by a black bandana. Nat swallowed. There was just something about a side braid.

Maddy watched him take away her masterpiece and then turned her head to greet the new customer who had arrived at her station: Nat Chambers. She shook her head and smiled. "You came," she said cheerfully as she wiped her hands on a nearby towel.

"Well you said huckleberries so how could I stay away?" Nat joked. Her heart began to quicken it's beat in her chest. "By the way, what's a huckleberry?"

Maddy leaned across the island, their hands wonderfully close. "I'm so glad you're here. I had a really nice time with you yesterday and I felt so stupid that I didn't ask for your number. I was worried that I might not see you again."

"Well, I wasn't about to let that happen."

"I get off in an hour…keep me company?"

"I was hoping you'd say that. I'd love to."

Maddy lit up and drummed her fingers on the island. "You hungry?"

"Always." She smiled. "I too have a sweet tooth and I heard the pastry chef here is pretty amazing. Any recommendations?"

Maddy giggled. "Yeah, I think I can arrange something special." She began creating the most beautifully elaborate dessert Nat had ever seen. Maddy's hands were magic as she whipped and whisked, sliced and arranged. She placed the plate in front of Nat, who sat slack jawed at the presentation.

"It's stunning."

"No, it's huckleberry," laughed Maddy. "This is an entrement of huckleberry with pomegranate and orange blossom crème. It's served with a huckleberry gastrique and a cannel of brown sugar gelato. It's kind of my version of a deconstructed huckleberry pie."

"You are amazing. I mean, it's amazing." She blushed at her own forwardness.

Maddy blushed in return and gestured for her to try it. "Try to get a little of everything on the spoon."

She complied and put a masterful spoonful in her mouth. She closed her eyes as it covered her taste buds. Sweet, rich, and tart all at the same time. She imagined this was what it was like to kiss Maddy and her skin erupted into goose bumps. She looked into Maddy's eyes and simply responded, "Mmm."

Maddy smiled broadly, looking pleased with herself.

Throughout the next hour, the two exchanged flirtatious small talk while Maddy attended to the other desserts. As Maddy's shift ended, she shook hands with a few of the guests and mouthed to Nat, "one second" before she disappeared behind a set of swinging doors. A few moments later she reappeared, her hair uncovered, wearing a pair of blue corduroys and a white Henley top that hugged her frame perfectly. She called behind her, "Night, guys!"

A chorus of, "Night, Chef!" followed her out the door.

It was still quite chilly at night but Nat actually found it refreshing. Between the warm restaurant and her skin being constantly flushed in Maddy's presence, the cool air was a welcome relief.

Maddy turned to Nat, a bit of a swing in her step. "Thank you for coming in tonight. I was really excited to see you sitting there. I don't suppose you'd be willing to walk a girl home? I only live a few blocks away."

"It would be my pleasure," Nat eagerly responded, offering her arm.

They passed a small hole-in-the-wall Mexican restaurant, and Maddy asked, "Have you ever been there before?" Nat shook her head no. "They have the most amazing margaritas and salsa you'll want to absolutely bathe in. Maybe I can take you there sometime."

"I would like that. It's been a while since I had a bath, so I'm down."

She laughed and squeezed Nat's arm tighter as they walked. They passed a few bars, rowdy patrons enjoying the cool, spring night.

A slightly intoxicated girl saw Nat and leaned over to her friend and whispered loudly, "Holy shit, I think that's Nat Chambers."

Nat gave the girl a quick nod, then returned her attention to Maddy, who pointed out a few other choice haunts in the neighborhood. She came to a stop in front of a nicely maintained, yet unassuming apartment building.

"This is me," she declared with an exaggerated sweeping motion of her arm. She took a step closer to Nat and reached her hand into Nat's pocket, pulling out her phone. Nat's pulse jumped. Maddy proceeded to type her number into the phone. "And this is also me," she said, handing the phone back to Nat. Their fingers touched as they passed the phone and Nat could feel the electricity between them like a static charge.

"Thanks," she managed to squeak.

"I googled you," Maddy said softly. "When you told me your name, I thought it sounded familiar. So, I looked you up. And you…" She lifted her hand and gently prodded Nat in the shoulder with her index finger. "…are some kind of famous musician, aren't you?"

"The level of my celebrity has been greatly exaggerated. I'm just a girl with a guitar who got lucky. Most people don't recognize me anyway."

"That girl outside the bar did." Maddy smiled and ran her hand down the length of Nat's leather jacket.

"Ahh, you caught that then?"

"Uh huh." Maddy stepped even closer, her eyes flashing between Nat's lips and her eyes. Nat felt an ache in the back of her throat, and she closed the space between them.

"Can I see you again?" Nat whispered. Maddy answered her with a soft kiss on the cheek.

"Here, this is for you." Maddy handed Nat a small, paper bag. "This is what I make for the staff. It's my favorite recipe. If you want to get to know me, then this is a good start. Forget about all the technique and elaboration. No matter what I do, or where I go, this is who I really am deep down." She touched the side of Nat's face. "Good night."

With that, Maddy turned, bounced up the steps and disappeared through the doors of the building. Nat held the paper bag in her trembling hand as she began walking toward the subway. She reached inside, and there was one, still warm, chocolate chip cookie. She lifted it to her lips and bit down on the chewy, crispy goodness. She could taste the butter and brown sugar, the chocolate melting on her tongue. It was so beautiful in its simplicity, crafted with absolute care. It was the best damn cookie she'd ever tasted. She bounded down the subway steps, a sugar rush of adrenaline carrying her.

CHAPTER ELEVEN

Over the next few days, Nat and Maddy texted and chatted on the phone. Maddy was unveiling a new menu at the restaurant and was swamped, and Nat was trying to get all of her ducks in a row before the Euro tour was upon her. While the women didn't see each other, they flirted and kept up with each other with texts and phone calls. Nat told her bandmates all about the beautiful chef, and they teased her for her apparently endearing clumsiness.

Then one morning Nat woke up with a tickle in her throat. It was a familiar feeling, one she knew and dreaded. A couple hours later at rehearsals, she began to get hoarse. By evening her voice was reduced to a barely audible squeak. She had acute laryngitis.

The next day also happened to be her twenty-ninth birthday. She couldn't help but wonder if this was some psychosomatic response to growing older and still not feeling completely in control of her future. Whatever the reason, she canceled her birthday dinner with Paul, Jackie and their friends, and turned off the ringer of her phone. If she was going to wallow, she was going to do it properly. She and Eddie burrowed themselves into the couch and fell asleep, *Antiques Roadshow* playing softly in the background.

She woke with a start when Eddie unceremoniously used her as a springboard. She rubbed her eyes and realized there was a soft knock at the door. *Damn it, Paul.* She got up, running her hands through her hopeless hair. She undid the latch and much to her surprise, there stood Maddy, shopping bags in her hands. Nat opened her mouth to speak, but Maddy lifted her hand.

"No, you don't have to say a word. Paul told me all about it." Nat looked at her curiously.

As if reading Nat's mind, Maddy continued. "Paul and Jackie showed up at the restaurant last night to catch a late dinner and told me you weren't feeling well. And that today is your birthday...which you neglected to mention. I thought I'd stop by and check on you. Paul told me where you lived. So, this isn't technically creepy, right?"

She started to laugh, covering her mouth when a squeak escaped. Maddy smiled a hopeful smile at her. "So, here I am. With things!" She lifted her bags. "Happy birthday Nat. Can I come in?"

She gestured for Maddy to enter and she breezed in and set her bags on the coffee table. "Here," she said as she pulled a small, white dry erase board out of one of the bags. "It's so you can write what you want to say because I'm a terrible lip reader. Can you have wine?" she asked, holding up a bottle of delicious Malbec.

Nat scribbled away and lifted the board to Maddy. *I don't see why not.* She signed it with a smiley face.

"Great, because this stuff is amazing. I swiped it from the back bar. Don't tell anyone." Maddy lifted a finger to her lips.

Beautiful and a rebel.

Maddy bit her lip and continued riffling through her bag. "It's not much, but I just don't think it's right to have a birthday without a birthday cake." She pulled out a small, simply decorated chocolate cake with the words *Happy Birthday Natalia* on it. "Ooh, and I have candles too!"

Nat looked at the cake and then looked at Maddy, and her heart set to bursting.

"Your first name is Natalia, right? I double checked with Paul, but I was worried he was pulling my leg."

The pen squeaked across the board. *Yes, It's Natalia. Hardly anyone calls me that, but I like the way it sounds when you say it.*

"Good, because I like the way it sounds when I say it. Like a secret. Something special." Maddy looked at her, and for a moment, she thought she should stride across the living room and kiss her. Her nerves got the best of her, though, and she stayed near the arm of the couch. Eddie swooped in to sniff and survey Maddy, who crouched down to greet him and scratch his chin. He purred and threw himself at her feet.

Wow! He hates everyone but me.

Maddy rubbed Eddie's belly and said, "Well, then look who made a new friend tonight."

Maddy grabbed two wineglasses hanging from a shelf in the kitchen and made her way to the couch and poured them each a healthy glassful. They sat next to each other, Nat's knee almost pressing against Maddy's. Maddy took the lead, telling stories about the restaurant, the craziness that happens behind the scenes. She asked Maddy simple questions, ones she could answer easily via the board.

"How long have you been playing guitar?"

Since I was twelve. My parents made me take piano. Hated it. But learned a lot. Begged for a guitar. Got one and never put it down.

"What's your background? I mean, Chambers... What's that?"

Brazilian on my mom's side. Dad's English and Scottish. You?

Maddy tugged at a red curl. "Well, Irish, which I'm sure comes as a total shocker, and French. When did you know you were..."

Gay?

"Ha, you're getting fast with that. Well I didn't want to assume how you labeled yourself, if at all."

I'm fine with gay, lesbian, queer. Smiley face. *Seventeen.*

Maddy smiled a sad smile. "Same sort of. I think I always knew. Even from a young age, but it was a secret I held very close."

Now two glasses of wine in, Nat twirled a strand of Maddy's curly red hair between her fingers. She moved her hand across Maddy's beautiful face and traced her jawline, her lips, and the bridge of her nose. Maddy closed her eyes and exhaled deeply, which caused Nat's stomach to knot in the best possible way. She ran her thumb across the small, white scar that ran through Maddy's eyebrow, and she shivered in response.

How did you get that scar?

Maddy was silent for a bit, and Nat became nervous that she had made Maddy uncomfortable. Maddy picked up her wineglass and took a long sip. "I grew up in a small town in Montana. It wasn't exactly the ideal place for a little lesbian growing up. I did my best to stay under the radar. More importantly, my father's radar. I got good grades, I went to church three times a week, and I worked every summer from the age of fourteen, saving and scrimping to go to college. I always wanted to cook, to bake. I loved the mathematics of it, the consistency. I found it very grounding. My father was..." She tapped on the sides of her wineglass. "...is...very religious. My mom died when I was young, so he raised me.

"The summer after high school, I was working at the local ice cream shop and I fell in love with one of my coworkers. She was kind and funny, played on the softball team. And she was brave, oh, so fucking brave. She didn't care who knew about her, so she told some of her friends about us. It ended up getting back to my Dad, and one night when I got back from a late night making ice cream sundaes and making out with her in the walk-in, my father was waiting for me. He was sitting in his armchair, the one no one else was allowed to sit in. 'A man's house is his castle' and all that nonsense. He asked me if I had sinned against our Lord. I told him that no, I had not because in my heart, I knew I hadn't. He got out of his chair and walked toward me and asked me again. 'Madeline, have you sinned against this family and our Lord?' I began to cry. He told me that he'd spoken to my girlfriend's parents and that I was no longer permitted to see her, under any circumstances. I felt my legs weaken beneath me and I wept in the middle of our living room. When I managed to find the words, I told him God loved me and had made me in his image. That was when he slapped me."

Nat's heart squeezed in her chest, and she moved her hand to Maddy's, hoping to comfort her.

"He wore this big, gold class ring, and it sliced my forehead open when he hit me. I couldn't see. So much blood ran into my eyes. I walked into my room and packed what I could, including my passport. After he went to sleep, I left the house and I've never been back. I emptied my bank account, all the money I'd saved over summers and graduation gifts. I hitched a ride to the airport with a friend and I bought a one-way ticket to Paris. It just seemed so impulsive and romantic at the time, the perfect place to start a new life, you know?" Nat nodded. "So, I arrived the next day at Charles de Gaulle Airport. Oh, did I mention I didn't speak a lick of French?"

Nat laughed silently and scribbled on her pad. *C'est dommage.*

Maddy smiled back. "Well, I certainly know it now. I rented a room in the 10th arrondissement from a sweet, middle-aged couple that owned a patisserie on the ground floor. After waking up day after day, smelling fresh croissants, I took it as a sign. I asked the husband if I could become his apprentice. He laughed at first. Here I was, a Midwestern girl who barely knew *en haut* from *en bas*. He eventually let me, and I learned everything you could imagine about pastry and bread. I enrolled in courses at the Institute Culinarie and became an official pastry chef. While I loved Paris and miss it terribly, I decided to try my luck in New York and eventually I made my way to Touché." Maddy stopped and covered her face with her hands. "Oh my god, I think I just told you my life story and you didn't even ask."

Nat took Maddy's hands from her face and held them in her own. Maddy's eyes sparkled with life and Nat just wanted to gaze into them forever. Instead, she dragged her marker across the board and turned it for Maddy to see. *You are the bravest person I've ever met. This is the best birthday ever.*

Maddy laughed and her eyes welled with tears. "Ahhh." She wiped her eyes. "We haven't even blown out your candles yet." She leaped from the couch and soon brought over the cake, gleaming with small, white candles. She held it in front of Nat and whispered, "Make a wish."

Nat did, and it was the biggest, warmest wish she'd ever made. She blew out the candles and watched the smoke curl around Maddy's face, making her look like a long-ago heroine rising through the mists. Maddy rustled through her bag and handed her a small, wrapped rectangle. Nat motioned that it wasn't necessary, but Maddy insisted. Nat unwrapped the package to reveal a copy of *Strangers in Paradise, Volume 1*. She could hardly contain her glee.

"I remember reading in an interview, that *Strangers in Paradise* was one of your biggest influences, but you had lost all your volumes over the years. So, here's a little something to start anew."

Maddy looked into her eyes again, and Nat mouthed, "Thank you."

They were drawn together like a magnet. From within Nat's throat rose a tickle that she couldn't contain, and she had to turn her head and cough. *I'm so sorry*, she hurriedly scribbled.

"Don't worry about it." Maddy shrugged it off. "How about we watch TV or something? Maybe *Trauma University* is on," she said with a knowing smile.

Nat tried not to laugh and pathetically nodded. Maddy motioned for her to move closer and rest her head against her shoulder. She obliged and shortly after some channel surfing, she fell sweetly, blissfully asleep on Maddy's shoulder.

She woke to the early sun poking through the shades of her living room. She was alone. She looked all around for Maddy, but she was gone. On the coffee table lay the white board, with the words, "Sweet dreams, birthday girl. Feel better soon, because your voice is becoming one of my favorite sounds. See you soon. Maddy."

She laid herself back on the couch as Eddie chirped and hopped up to join her. Maybe twenty-nine wouldn't be so bad, she thought. She drifted back to sleep, a smile on her lips.

CHAPTER TWELVE

A few days later Nat was back in fighting shape. During her recovery, she and Maddy had exchanged dozens of texts as Nat lay on the couch, sipping on strong ginger tea and binge-watching British crime dramas. With her voice back, albeit a little scratchy, she was ready to talk again and get on with prepping for the tour, and more urgently, seeing Maddy again.

"Hey there!" Maddy said with excitement. "Wait, can you talk, or will this just be a heavy breathing sort of thing?"

She laughed into the receiver. "No, sorry to disappoint. I can speak again. But I can do a little heavy breathing if you like."

"Hmm, that's tempting, but your froggy voice is making me all kinds of happy now."

She could hear the sounds of pots and pans clanking in the background. "Oh shit, did I get you at a bad time? Are you like elbow deep in a soufflé or something? I couldn't bear it if I was responsible for the destruction of a soufflé."

"Nat Chambers, you are funny. And no, you are no soufflé murderer. Actually, come to think of it, I haven't made a soufflé since pastry school. Don't tell anyone but I think they're overrated."

"Your culinary confession is safe with me, Chef."

"Actually, I'm just putting in my orders for the week. What are you up to?"

Her stomach began to flutter. "Well, I was going to see if you wanted to get some lunch with me, maybe at that little Mexican joint you raved about."

"That sounds pretty amazing. I can be done here in an hour and can steal away for a bit before we start prepping for service tonight."

"Great, so I'll see you then." She smiled at the good news and ran to her closet to find something that screamed, *I'm effortlessly cool and not at all awkward around women I like.*

She grabbed a vintage Dolly Parton shirt she had fought a hard-won battle for on eBay. One look at her hair told her it was a hat day, so she dug out her best black beanie before picking up her keys and rushing out the door.

It was a blessedly warm day and when she got to the restaurant, Maddy was already seated outside on the mix-matched patio. She waved a hand and Nat had to take a deep breath. She wore a plain white T-shirt and a pair of houndstooth chef pants, with her hair in a high ponytail. In other words, completely and utterly adorable.

Maddy stood up to hug Nat as she approached, and Nat took in the warmth of her touch and the clean scent of her skin. When they pulled away from each other, Nat instantly missed the weight of Maddy in her arms.

"You know," she remarked as she gave Maddy an exaggerated once over, "You have somehow totally changed my feelings on the subject of Crocs. You make them look amazing."

Maddy playfully modeled her footwear. "These are the shoes of champions. Have you ever tried to get raspberry coulis out of a pair of Uggs or Nikes? No, it's a Sisyphean task. Well, I just spray these babies down with warm water and boom! I'm ready to take on the world."

"You are something else, Madeline. I bow before your awesome." She motioned for Maddy to sit. They settled in and she reached for one of the sticky menus, but Maddy leaned close and traced her finger across Nat's hand. She glanced down at her long, tapered fingers and noticed little pink and brown scars scattered. They were chef's hands, with nicks from sharp knives, burns from too hot pans, and splatters of molten sugar. She wanted to kiss every inch of them.

"Do you trust me?" Maddy asked, breaking Nat from her trance.

"Uh, yes, of course."

"Then we don't need menus." Maddy smiled. She motioned to the waitress. "Hey Luisa, can you ask Chef to send us out some of his favorites? Oh, and a giant bowl of your salsa and chips, and two Mexican Coca-Colas, please."

Luisa kindly nodded and headed back inside.

Maddy leaned back and bit lightly on her lip. "I like your shirt."

Nat broke into a huge grin. The T-shirt was a good choice. "Queen Dolly. Only one of the finest songwriters and musicians ever to walk the earth. Have you ever seen her live?" Maddy shook her head, obviously delighting in Nat's enthusiasm. "Well, she's incredible. Like she can kick the ass of any musician half her age." She leaned in. "If you could distill the sun into ninety pounds and a platinum blond wig, you'd have Dolly."

Maddy let out a chuckle. "Wow, I hope someone describes me like that one day."

"Really? Because you are rocking the ginger thing. By the way, how long have you been Insta-famous?"

Maddy smiled. "Insta-famous? I am hardly Insta-famous."

"I did a little social media stalking. Twenty thousand followers. Not too shabby."

"Well, thank you. It didn't really start to pick up until after I moved to NYC."

"The pics are amazing. I really like the ones of you in your chef hat and coat. Something about those little hats just gets me right here." She lightly pounded her chest and swooned.

Maddy blushed.

"But seriously, @pastrygrlnyc, I'm really into it. I love that you share your recipes too. It feels like you're just talking to a friend when you're reading your posts."

"That's about the best compliment you could have given me," Maddy said. "Thank you."

She was caught in Maddy's stare for a moment and nearly had to shake herself out of it. "Hey, so the other night, what you shared with me… That was a big deal. I knew you were beautiful and really, really cool, but you're also strong. I want you to feel like you can share anything with me."

Maddy traced a finger along the wrought-iron design of the table. "You know, it's kind of weird because we only met recently, but I feel like I can share things with you. I look into your eyes and…"

They were interrupted when Luisa returned to the table with two ice-cold Cokes and a big bowl of chips and salsa. The serious talk would have to wait until after lunch.

"Nice. The chips are still warm," Nat exclaimed as she dipped a chip in the bright red salsa.

"I know." Maddy exclaimed as she chomped down on one herself.

"And the salsa…it's so…" Nat mumbled through a mouthful of chip.

"Amazing. I know." Maddy winked at her.

"We need a moment of silence to honor the deliciousness of these chips and salsa."

"You are kind of a dork. Did you know that?" Maddy asked, the smile on her face big and genuine.

Nat looked up at her. "You're just figuring this out? Don't let the rock star thing confuse you. Grade-A dork, here."

"Well, it's your lucky day, because I'm super into dorks, especially cute, talented dorks."

Now it was Nat's turn to blush. They continued to flirt and chat and soon Luisa brought by numerous aromatic small plates, each one more tempting and delicious than the one before.

They shared their food, and Maddy explained what each was: tamales with roasted pork and an earthy mole sauce, a bright ceviche with fresh avocado, and a hearty birria stew that Nat knew she would crave now on chilly winter nights.

"You like the goat, huh?" Maddy asked, already knowing the answer.

"What gave you that idea? Is it because I'm practically wearing it right now? Or the whispering of sweet nothings?"

"Well, both frankly." Maddy put down her spoon and stared into her bowl. "I could make this for you sometime if you like. Well, not as good as Chef's, but I'm not too shabby with the savory. Pastry might be my specialty but I'm a good cook too."

"I have no doubt, and that sounds amazing." Nat slid her hand over to Maddy's and interlocked their fingers. Maddy's warm hand felt like heaven.

"So, I told you my story the other night. Now it's your turn to tell me all your secrets, Nat Chambers." Maddy squeezed Nat's fingers.

She cleared her throat. "Huh. Okay, well I was born and raised in the Hudson Valley. My parents still live there. Dad's a librarian and aspiring mystery novelist. Mom's an interior designer. I inherited Dad's gift for written words and none of my mother's style."

Maddy chuckled. "I don't know about that. I thought your apartment was very chic."

"That's because she decorated it. I'm lucky if I walk out of the house in matching socks. Anyway, I went to college in Boston, Berklee College of Music. I majored in voice, but I really couldn't stand the rigidness of classical voice and opera, so I switched my major to songwriting my sophomore year."

"You can sing opera?" Maddy asked with a twinkle in her eye.

"Yes, I can and no I won't."

Maddy stuck out her bottom lip in a pout.

"Pout all you want. It makes your mouth look amazing."

"You are so cheeky."

"Anyway, from there I moved to Nashville for a couple years and I started writing music for myself and other musicians. You know, Annie Stevens, the alt-country singer?"

"Yes, I love her album, *Starlings*."

"Well, I wrote a few of those songs. 'Cry Havoc,' 'Starving,' and 'Wait for Me, My Darling.'"

Maddy clapped her hands and let out a little squeal. "'Wait for Me, My Darling' is my absolute favorite from that album. I can't believe I didn't know you wrote it."

"Well, songwriters don't always get a taste of the limelight, which is why I still perform my own music as well. Is that petty of me to admit? I love being on stage."

"No, I completely understand. Plus, you're so talented. I totally downloaded your latest album after we went out for coffee." Maddy flushed.

"Really?" She was touched. She liked the idea of Maddy listening to her voice and words as she baked at the restaurant or danced around her living room.

"Maddy, I really want to kiss you right now." She was surprised at her own boldness.

"Good, because I really, really want you to kiss me."

They leaned across the table, and as they came closer, Maddy's phone chimed.

"Damn it." She looked down at the phone. "It's one of my guys, and they know I'm on a date and will be murdered if it's not an emergency."

Nat waved sympathetically and sat back in her chair.

Maddy answered the call. "Hey. What's going on? Okay, so they got the entire shipment wrong?" She sighed. "Well, there's not much we can do except make an emergency run to the market. Call Marie and ask her to stay open as a favor to me. I'll be right there." She pursed her lips and slid the phone into her pocket. "I'm so sorry, Nat. There was a major fuckup and I have to do damage control."

"No apology necessary. You go do your chef thing and I'll take care of things here."

"Okay, but I get next time. Sound good?" Maddy said as she got up from her chair.

"Absolutely." Nat rose and before she knew it, Maddy stepped in and kissed her quickly on the lips.

"Goodbye, Nat. I had a great time," Maddy said softly, her lips still close to Nat's.

"Mmm," was all Nat could dreamily reply as Maddy took off down the street.

CHAPTER THIRTEEN

"Paul? Can you create a lower harmony for this line? It feels a little hollow with just Jackie and me."

The trio sat in their rehearsal space, plunking out harmonies and trying new sounds for the European tour. Now that Nat had fully recovered, it was back to work.

"How about this?" Paul sang a few notes and Nat nodded in approval.

"Yeah, that works. It fills that hole nicely."

Jackie and Paul began to giggle uncontrollably at this statement. Jackie even fell off her chair. Nat, knowing she'd just set herself up for this reaction, joined in. "We are a mature lot, aren't we?"

"What are you ladies doing tonight?" Paul asked, wiping a tear of laughter from his eye "I mean besides filling your holes."

"Oh man, you are a sick puppy," Nat replied. "Uh, I was thinking of trying to meet up with Maddy."

Paul and Jackie looked at each other, then Nat, and smiled. "Well, guess who is coming to town tonight and playing a surprise show at Haven?"

Jackie and Nat both shrugged.

"Redfern."

Nat slapped her hand on her knee and grinned. Redfern used to play a lot of the same venues as the Nat Chambers Band back in the day and they were on the same label. They had all become good friends over the years. The guys in Redfern had relocated to Austin in the last year, and this was a very pleasant surprise.

"Yeah, Steve called me last night. He, Dan, Ari, and Andy are doing a few East Coast shows to promote their new album. Anyway, they'd love to see you, Nat. They are really excited to hear your new music which I told them was a thing that existed and not just in our dreams, Chambers."

Nat glared at him. "Oh, thanks."

"And I'm sure Steve would love to meet you, Jackie."

Jackie cocked her eyebrow. "What's this Steve feller like?"

"He's got a handlebar mustache and really tight jeans," Paul answered.

"Sold." She twirled one of Paul's nearby drumsticks.

"So, what do you say, Nat? I'm buying the drinks." He looked up at her with hopeful eyes.

"Well hell, I can't miss an evening with Redfern. Yes, I'm in. What do you think about me texting Maddy to see if she'd like to join us? I kind of feel like we are there now. You know, getting to know the friends." She pulled out her phone, just as Paul's phone chirped. He looked down at it.

"No need," he responded. "She said yes, and she can't wait to see you."

"What the actual hell, Paul? You already talked to her?"

"Oh, we text. We're like, text buddies now. I think she's really sprung on you. By the way, Redfern may ask us to play with them, so be ready. I need to vape. Be right back."

Nat looked at Jackie with exasperation. Jackie opened her mouth to speak.

"I remember my first handlebar mustache. It was a dead sexy Aussie hipster I met on holiday. It tickles so good."

Nat just looked at her.

"What?" Jackie responded innocently while twirling an invisible mustache.

"I'm curious. Do you have a type?"

"Yes. Hot boys with mustaches."

She loved the way Jackie said mustaches in her British accent, like moostashes. "Well, that narrows down the field."

"Are you implying I'm shallow? Because I'm not shallow. I once dated a guy with zero fashion sense. He had a really great arse, though."

"I heard great arse. Quit talking about me when I'm not in the room." Paul leaned back in, smelling of sweet vapor.

"No, I was telling Nat about the guy I dated with the mom jeans."

"Oh yeah, I saw pics. He did have a great ass, though."

"Natalia here thinks I'm a shallow slutty slut."

"Shallow is a bit harsh," Paul added.

"Thank you." Jackie slapped him on the knee.

"Wait, I didn't call anyone shallow. Or a slut. I would never slut-shame. I'm all for sexual expression," Nat said. "I prefer to think of both of you as free-spirited, especially in your pants."

"Amen," Paul said, raising his hands to the sky. "So, speaking of slutting it up… Sorry, 'expressing oneself sexually.' You and Maddy? Have you gone there yet?"

Nat blushed furiously. "Well, why don't you ask Maddy, since you guys are BFFs now?"

He leaned back in a big stretch. "Oh, I already did. She just responded by sending me an emoji of a unicorn and a middle finger."

Nat wanted to be mad at him, but she couldn't help the laugh that escaped her. Something about Maddy's response to him made Nat like her even more. "Not that it's any of your business."

"Is it any of *my* business?" asked Jackie who was now flipping through a *Rolling Stone*.

"No. It's not any of your business either. But since you asked, no, we have not gone there yet. We haven't even really kissed yet."

"What?" Jackie and Paul shouted in unison.

"We are taking it slow. She's just so fun and lovely. There hasn't been a perfect moment." Nat picked at an already frayed spot on the knee of her jeans.

Paul reached over and put his hand on Nat's shoulder. "Honey, there are no perfect moments. But it's sweet of you to think that. I say take the girl into the nearest dark corner. It's about time you got past this Melissa thing."

"Yes, because nothing says I want to have gaybies with you like a filthy fingerbang," Jackie interjected. "You, my darling Paul, are an idiot. Lesbians are gentle creatures with emotional needs."

Nat cocked her head and knitted her eyebrows at Jackie. "Since when are you the Jane Goodall of lesbians?"

"I watched a documentary. Okay, so it was on koalas, but it made me think about lesbians." She shrugged good-naturedly.

"You are both out of your heads. If you don't mind, I'd like to handle this my own way. And Paul, I am over the Melissa thing."

"Really? Because according to Oliver you had an absolute meltdown at the suggestion of going on tour with Melissa again."

Paul's words cut through Nat like a hot knife. First, she was angry that Oliver had shared the details of their meeting, but they were after all, The Nat Chambers Band. Paul and Jackie were just as invested in their success as Nat was. Then the reality of Paul's suggestion, that she wasn't really over Melissa washed over her. If she was truly over Melissa, would she have agreed to go on tour? Or was self-preservation her right no matter?

"Would you really want to go on tour with Melissa again, Paul?" Nat snapped.

"No, he doesn't," Jackie added. "She sounds like an absolute twat, Paul. Why are you pushing this issue?"

"I'm just trying to figure out where your head is, Chambers. I don't want you marching into something you aren't ready for. I'm looking out for you."

"You want to know where my head is? Just watch." She pulled out her phone and texted Maddy about the show and how she couldn't wait to see her. Maddy responded with a unicorn emoji and a thumbs up. Followed by a heart. Nat smiled and showed the texts to Paul and Jackie, trying to prove the point to Paul. She then rose and took her place in front of the rehearsal mic. She swung her guitar across her chest as Paul and Jackie set themselves up as well.

"Okay, let's try 'Damned if I Do' again. Jackie, please give me two choruses at the end, okay? Paul, can you count us off?"

He clicked his sticks together.

CHAPTER FOURTEEN

Nat arrived at Haven, where she was recognized by Tim the bouncer. He gave her a big squeeze that lifted her clear off the ground. "Looking good, Nat," he said mid hug.

Truth be told, she had gone through four outfits before she decided on a well-worn and fitted pair of Levi's, a black V-neck and collarless leather jacket. At least Tim liked it.

"Flatterer," she playfully responded as he ushered her past the crowd gathered outside.

Inside the club young and attractive hipsters milled around with glasses of whiskey and cans of High Life. At the end of the bar stood Paul, Jackie, and Maddy. Nat felt the air rush out of her when she saw Maddy, a drink in her hand, her head thrown back laughing at something Paul said. She looked stunning in a simple vintage forest green dress that perfectly complemented her hair and hazel eyes. Paul caught sight of Nat and waved her over. Maddy smiled as Nat neared and greeted her with a tight hug and kiss on the cheek. She smelled faintly of rum and coconut shampoo, and Nat wanted to breathe her in all night.

"Hi." Nat took a step back to admire her up close. "You look…incredible."

Maddy bit her lip to help stifle a smile. She tugged on Nat's jacket and pulled her close. "And you look like a goddamn rock star tonight," she whispered in Nat's ear, brushing her lips against Nat as she pulled back. Nat swallowed hard as she felt a jolt in her jeans.

"So, what are you drinking?" Nat motioned to Maddy's glass.

She swirled the brown liquid and ice and offered it to Nat. "Mt. Gay Manhattan. The mixologists here are top notch. They even make their own bitters. Try it."

Nat took a small sip of the sweet and strong cocktail.

Maddy leaned in closer. "I already ate the cherry," she said, causing Nat to choke on the liquor.

Maddy giggled. "You okay?" Nat nodded. "Sorry, this drink is really strong. What was I thinking? I practically get drunk off the smell of vanilla extract."

Nat took Maddy's hand and interlocked their fingers. "It's totally cool. Have fun. I'll make sure you get home safely."

Maddy perked up. "So, no slumming it on the F line?" Nat shook her head. Maddy leaned in and gave her a quick but wonderfully soft kiss on the lips. Before Nat's head even had a chance to swim, she was interrupted by a tap on her shoulder. She turned to see her old friend Steve from Redfern. They embraced and Steve fist-bumped Paul.

"Goddamn, you guys got old!" Steve observed before Nat punched him lightly in the shoulder.

"It's only been two years and we look fucking flawless," responded Paul as he gave Steve's mustache a pull. "Oh, Steve, speaking of fucking flawless… This is our bandmate, Jackie Adeyemi. She's from London. Plays a mean cello."

Steve extended his hand to Jackie, and as their hands met, it had to have been obvious to everyone in a ten-mile radius that sparks were flying. "Jackie Adeyemi from London, it's a real pleasure. We've got to hit the stage, but I'd love to talk to you after the show. Will you stick around?"

Jackie demurred and flashed him her million-dollar smile. "Yeah, sure. I'll be here." Steve kissed her hand and walked toward the stage, while Jackie watched him go. "Good god, those pants are tight," she observed.

"Told you," Paul replied, tossing back the remainder of his drink.

Nat, who got a big kick out of the whole exchange, ordered another round and settled in with Maddy to watch the show. She slipped her hand around Maddy's waist, and Maddy leaned against her in response. She thought about Maddy's warm skin just below her fingertips, wishing there was no barrier between them.

The pulsing of the kick drum roused her from her daydream as Redfern launched into their first song. The band was tight, more together than Nat remembered. Maybe getting the hell out of Dodge was just what the guys had needed. The crowd ate them up. Nat and Maddy swayed and rocked to the beat and Paul mouthed the words to one of their songs. With each song, Nat and Maddy found new ways to touch each other. A caress on the cheek, a nuzzle to the neck, hands on thighs and the small of a back. Soon enough, the electricity between them could barely be contained. Nat took Maddy's chin in her hand and pulled her in for a slow kiss. She brushed her tongue against Maddy's lower lip and Maddy welcomed her. It could have gone on forever if Nat had her way, except for the jarring sound of Steve's voice over the microphone.

"It's great to be back home! You are all fucking gorgeous. For the love of god, keep drinking! There are a few special folks in the audience tonight, and I want to invite them to join us on stage. Ladies and gents, The Nat Chambers Band!"

As the audience erupted into cheers, Nat felt Paul's hands grab her shoulders and pull her toward the stage. She looked back at Maddy, who was clapping and smiling from ear to ear. When they got on stage, Steve passed Nat his electric guitar. Paul joined Ari at the drum kit, and Steve motioned to Jackie to join him at his mic. Steve covered the mic with his hands and shouted over to Nat.

"How about 'Speak'? I know the harmonies for that one and Andy knows the bass line." Nat blew a kiss to Andy and nodded to Steve. Paul and Ari counted them in and the audience responded with whoops and cheers to the familiar opening chords. Nat's fingers flew across the guitar as she leaned into the mic.

You speak in tongues and every one of them lies.
You say my name, and every part of me dies.
I just want you to tell the truth, to want me back, to face me
But you don't and you won't and can't and it breaks me!

She growled the chorus and Steve and Jackie joined in on harmonies. Paul was wailing away on the kit, while Ari switched to hand percussion. Andy laid down a stellar bass line, and for a moment Nat wished she had stolen him away from Redfern back in the day. The audience bopped their heads and spilled their drinks as they danced. She caught sight of Maddy, who had come closer to the stage, her eyes as big as saucers, smiling wide. She crouched during the chorus, took Maddy's hand and kissed it before returning to the mic to sing the bridge.

All the times I couldn't speak,
You said that I was so damn weak,
But now I know what you're about,
Now I don't have a single doubt.

Both bands kicked it up through the final chorus, and afterward, the audience went crazy. The Nat Chambers Band took their bows and exited the stage.

Maddy greeted Nat when she stepped offstage and wordlessly wrapped her arms around Nat's waist. Some fans came up to Nat, and Maddy graciously stepped aside to let them get in a few words.

After the crowd cleared, Nat took Maddy's hand. "You wanna get some air?" she asked.

Maddy nodded and they stepped out of the club. Paul was standing outside smoking with a handsome man in a tight T-shirt and vintage jeans. He gave Nat a wink. Nat led Maddy to an empty piece of sidewalk where they could catch their breath. She was buzzing from the evening, the drinks, the performance, but mostly from Maddy. Her chest tightened at the image of Maddy twirling in that green dress.

Maddy's face shone under the East Village lamplight as she let out a giggle that turned into a small shriek. Nat laughed in response to her exuberance.

"That was the most amazing thing I've ever seen," Maddy declared, taking Nat's hands in her own.

Nat was used to compliments for her performances but hearing it from Maddy caused her cheeks to pink and her heart to race. "Thanks, I mean it wasn't my best. I'm pretty sure I was a little sharp on the last note and I nearly missed a key change during—"

"Stop! Nat Chambers, you blew me away. And you know what else?"

"What?"

"I'm going to kiss your stupidly talented mouth right now." Maddy closed the distance between them, reaching up and tugging a handful of Nat's hair as she pulled her closer in one quick move.

If Nat thought their first kiss in the bar was magical, this one transported her to a place she only felt when she was on stage, endorphins popping and a blissful light-headedness. Maddy made sweet little humming noises of approval as their lips passed over each other. Nat ran her tongue over Maddy's full bottom lip. It tasted of booze and beeswax, and she wanted more. As they were about to deepen the kiss, a high-pitched whistle pulled them both out of it. She snapped her head around to see Paul, now joined by Jackie and Steve. Paul had his fingers in whistle formation at his lips, while Jackie cuddled closer into Steve, who had his arm over the petite cellist.

"Traitors!" Nat shouted in their direction as they laughed and gave her the thumbs-up. "Sorry about my friends. They are beautiful assholes."

"Natalia?" Maddy grabbed lightly at Nat's jacket again.

"Yeah?"

"I'm kind of...a little..." whispered Maddy.

"Yeah?" Nat leaned in closer.

"Tipsy," laughed Maddy as she put her hand to her head with embarrassment.

"Well, those Manhattans pack a punch."

"I might be a little drunk on that kiss too. I had an amazing time tonight. You're something very special and if I don't go home right now, I won't stop kissing you."

"Is that such a bad thing?" Nat asked with a twinkle in her eye.

Maddy suddenly got a serious look on her face, and lifted her hand to Nat's face, tracing the line of Nat's lip with her thumb.

"Yeah, it would be, because I think there's something special here and I want to savor it. Is that okay?" Maddy's fingertips fell heavily onto Nat's jacket.

She was a bit taken aback. Maddy was saying exactly what she was feeling, and it was weird. But weird in the best possible way. "Yes, that's more than okay," she assured her and placed a small, sweet kiss on her forehead.

"Can I see you later this week?" Maddy asked.

"Absolutely. Let's get you a cab back to your place, okay?"

Maddy nodded and slipped her fingers through Nat's as she lifted her other hand to hail a cab.

Savor. What a perfectly perfect word, Nat decided.

CHAPTER FIFTEEN

Nat's finger hovered above the send button on her phone. What was she so nervous about? It was just a text, and Maddy was just a human. No, she was an angel food cake come to life topped with delicate powdered sugar and full of wit and charm. Now she even had Nat thinking in baking analogies.

Her phone contained a message from Maddy. *Had a blast the other night. Wanna hang out for a bit before I head into work?*

Nat badly wanted to hang out, but she had to get her ass into the studio and get in some practice and writing time before Paul and Jackie joined her. *I have to practice at the studio today. Wanna come?*

Why not combine the best of both worlds? In addition to being a star baker and an incredible kisser, maybe she knew how to play piano, Nat reasoned. "Ah fuck it." She hit send. A few moments later, the familiar three dots appeared on the screen.

Would love to. What's the address?

She swallowed hard. Her lips still tingled and she was flush between her thighs from their kiss the night before, but she needed to keep her cool if she was going to show Maddy she was serious about her.

Serious. Was she even ready to be serious? Sure, it had been almost a year since things imploded with Melissa, but she'd had a bitter taste in her mouth for so long. She swirled her tongue behind her teeth because for her betrayal was a tangible flavor. She quickly realized that it no longer lingered there like the stale metallic taste of old pennies. There was nothing there now. Yeah, it was time to move on.

"This place is the coolest!" Maddy declared as Nat gave her a tour of the Queens studio where she and the band rehearsed weekly.

Nat hadn't given it much thought, but it was a pretty cool space. Autographed pictures adorned the walls, while guitars and basses hung from hooks and rested in stands around the room. There was a red stand-up piano with names carved in the fading paint. Maddy seemed particularly drawn to it, as she ran her fingers over the crudely chiseled names.

"Redfern," she read out loud.

"Well you know them now."

"The Fiery Ones."

"Cool name, terrible band."

Maddy moved her finger and laughed, looking at Nat. "The Moaning Pickles?"

"Terrible name, surprisingly good band if you are into xylophones."

"Amazing," Maddy said with a smile. "I'm going to have to look them up for sure. Do you play," Maddy motioned to the piano, "or just guitar?"

"Yeah, I mean, I'm no Tori Amos or anything," Nat said as she sat down at the piano. "Enough to plunk out notes and arrange. I also play the bass, trumpet, and banjo."

"Banjo? Really?"

Nat sighed. "We all went through a banjo phase in the mid-aughts. I blame Mumford and Sons. I actually blame Mumford and Sons for a lot of things."

"Sounds like you are really good with your hands, then." Maddy smiled which made Nat blush something fierce. She thought Maddy looked especially cute in a pair of ripped jeans and a plain white T. If she didn't stop thinking about the way the jeans hung on Maddy's curvy hips, she was going to burst.

"Not to brag or anything," she said as she placed her hands on the keys, "but I have perfect pitch."

Maddy cocked her head to the side and looked at Nat with curious eyes.

"Really?"

She nodded.

"Is that your big pick-up line with the ladies?"

"No, I've actually never tried it before. Did it work?"

"Yes. Okay, Captain Rock Star…prove it." Maddy gave her a poke in the ribs.

"Pick a key, any key. Just don't push it down yet," she encouraged.

Maddy chose a key near the bottom on the keyboard.

"Well, not that key. I'm not really a bass," Nat giggled. "Something in this area.

She motioned to the center of the keyboard.

Maddy reached across her, giving her instant goose bumps, and picked a note. "Good ol' C five. Okay." She let out a sustained note and looked back at Maddy. "Now play it."

Maddy pushed down on the key and the note was exactly as Nat had sung it. "Huh. That's pretty freaking cool. Is this a trick?"

Nat shook her head. "No, try another one." Maddy reached across again and picked a higher note.

"D sharp six. Good thing I warmed up," she said with confidence before letting out the high note in her upper register.

Maddy slapped her hands on her knees. "How do you do that?"

She shrugged. "I honestly don't know. Maybe it's because I've been into music my whole life. Just one of those unexplainable things. It's fun to whip out at parties."

"Well." Maddy leaned into her. "I think it's really amazing. I think *you* are really amazing."

Nat's chest felt like it was full of helium, and she wasted no time in meeting Maddy's lips with her own. They kissed hard and fast. She took Maddy's hips in her hands and pulled her closer, moving her to a sitting position on the piano keyboard while Nat stood between her legs. The notes clanged out as Maddy wrapped her ankles around Nat's knees and moved her hands to keep herself steady. Maddy's hand swept up her abdomen and was about to cup her breast when they were interrupted by laughter in the hall.

Nat would know Jackie's giggle and Paul's wheezing guffaw anywhere, so she and Maddy quickly disengaged as the pair reached the door. Jackie and Paul's laughter quickly turned to surprise when they saw Nat and Maddy, red-cheeked and out of breath. The duo looked at the women and then at each other and broke out into laughter again.

Nat smoothed her hair and shirt down and helped Maddy off the keyboard as they exchanged looks of mortification and pent-up desire.

Paul tugged at his dark beard. "Did we interrupt a private rehearsal? Nat, were you teaching Maddy about *aural* comprehension?"

Jackie elbowed him in the ribs, causing him to let out a peal of unexpected pain. Nat shot him the look of death.

"Aural means hearing, you shit."

"I know what I said." He grimaced.

"Hi Maddy, nice to see you again," Jackie interjected, making a small wave of her hand. "You'll need to excuse Paul. He's a right wanker when he's…Paul."

Maddy smiled back, then turned to Nat. "Thanks for inviting me to your studio. I really loved seeing where you work. Now when I'm daydreaming, I'll know where to picture you."

Nat let out an audible gasp as her heart nearly leapt out of her chest. "My schedule is pretty crazy this week, but I'll text you later, okay?" Maddy kissed her gently on the cheek.

"Yeah, okay," she responded breathlessly. She no longer cared about their audience as she leaned in and kissed Maddy softly on the lips, then walked her to the door. Maddy left, and once they could no longer hear her heels clicking on the wood floors, Nat allowed herself to melt into a puddle on the floor.

"Ho. Ly. Shit!" Jackie exclaimed.

"I feel like I just walked into an episode of *The L Word*," Paul declared. "You know back when Shane was wearing those hideous leather shirts. That's not a comment on your fashion choices. You were about to bang her!"

"Don't say bang, Paul!" Nat shouted. Then she demurred. "I don't know. Maybe. Seriously, don't ever say bang again."

Jackie plopped down in the comfy armchair she'd called dibs on since she joined the band. "That girl likes you, Nat. A lot."

She ran her hands through her hair. "I really like her too."

"Are we going to lesbian process now?" Paul asked as he tuned his drums. "I mean, I'm fine if that's what's happening. I just want to know if I should get us some hummus and pinot grigio."

Jackie rolled her eyes as Nat sighed. "No, no processing today. Rain check. We really need to work on this setlist and maybe write a new goddamn song before Oliver kills me."

"Okay, let's bang it out," Paul said with a smirk.

"Damn it, Paul!"

CHAPTER SIXTEEN

Nat stayed in the studio after Paul and Jackie packed up and left. Her fingers traveled up and down the keyboard as she hummed a melody to herself. She paused, picked up her pen and scribbled down some words that were floating around in her head.

I've seen the stars
I've choked on their dust
When you flew my way
I knew that I must...
Know your name. Know your name.

Thoughts of Maddy filled her head and she was in a space where she felt most comfortable as a writer. "Falling in love and falling apart are always the best times to write," a fellow songwriter had once told her, and she knew this to be true. She wasn't exactly on a tear, but it was something, and it felt better than all those months of stagnation. Maddy made her heart sing, and now her brain just needed to catch up and provide some lyrics. Just as she was about to head into a new verse, her phone sent a vibration through the piano. It was her mother.

"Hello, *Querida*!"

"Hi, Mom. How are you?"

"Oh, you know me. Busy, busy. Working on one of those big old homes in Buffalo now. The owner has done a real marvel with the house. I'll have to send you pictures."

"Sure, I'd love to see it. How's Dad?"

"Your father is your father. Nose in a book. I think he's starting to lose a little of his hearing."

"I think that's just called not listening, Mom."

Her mother laughed. "You're probably right. What am I thinking? The man has only been half listening to me since 1990. One time I told him I was going to run off with that Ryan Gosling, and he said, 'I'll take mine with cream.'"

"Sounds about right," Nat chuckled.

"Enough about your father. How are you, *meu bem*?"

"I'm fine, you know. Rehearsing. Writing. Well, trying to write."

"Have you found any inspiration? You were always like that. The muse has to come up and tap you on the head."

She let out a small dry laugh. Her mother knew her well. "Well, let's say there is definitely some musing happening."

"Really? Oh, Natalia! What's her name? Tell me all about her. Is she a musician?"

"Oh god no. No more musicians. She's a pastry chef, actually. A really good one."

"And her name?"

She sighed. "If I tell you, do you promise not to go around digging for the goods on her? You can be a bit of a bloodhound."

Her mother clucked her tongue. "Me? I'm insulted."

"You once found out what chair an ex-girlfriend was in middle school orchestra. You have your ways."

"Well, it is true I am excellent at this, but I promise to keep it to a minimum," her mother said, sounding genuine.

"Fine, her name is Maddy. Madeline LaDuke." She instantly knew it was a mistake as she heard her mother's fingers fly on her computer keyboard, followed by a hoot of excitement.

"Look at this beauty! A redhead no less. I don't know what's more gorgeous, her or her pastries."

"Well, so much for that promise."

"What? She's on Instagram. It wasn't exactly hard. Your mamma just wants to know if you are happy."

"I think so. Yeah. I am. I like her a lot," she said, her heart squeezing at the thought of Maddy.

"Well I am going to light a candle for you."

"You don't even go to church anymore, Mom."

"I'm Brazilian and Catholic, I'm always welcome in God's house to light a candle, even if my Catholicism has lapsed a bit. I miss you dearest. Come and visit me and your Dad soon, okay?"

"I will do my best, mãe."

"And bring the chef."

With that, her mother hung up and left Nat to stare at her notebook, plunking out notes and humming away.

CHAPTER SEVENTEEN

The next morning Nat opened her eyes to find Eddie staring at her from the top of her pillow. She wiped at her eyes as he swatted at her messy ponytail. "Yeah dude, I get it. You're hungry."

Eddie simply chirped and sauntered down the hall toward the kitchen, his belly swaying from side to side.

Nat fumbled for her phone and saw two messages waiting for her. The first was from Maddy. *Good morning, cute stuff.* The simple sweetness of it made Nat smile ear to ear.

The second message was from Oliver. *Call me as soon as you get up. And I mean as soon. Not after coffee and frozen waffles or whatever you have in that abyss of a fridge. This shit is time sensitive.*

Her lip curled but she shook the sleep off and dialed his number.

"Rise and shine, Nat." Oliver's voice was particularly peppy this morning. That usually meant he wanted Nat to do something.

"And good day to you. What's the emergency?"

"Got an email last night from QROK. They want you to fill in on Kelli K's show for a guest who cancelled last minute. It's at noon. Can you do it?"

While it sounded like a request, Nat knew it wasn't really. She didn't have much choice in the matter. Sometimes you had to schmooze and chat. It was part of the gig. "Kelli K. Sounds like…fun?"

"You haven't been on her show before?" he asked.

He'd only been her manager for the last two years so anything before that was pretty much a clusterfuck of random appearances and shady promoters. For as much as he nagged her, she knew he was a damn good manager.

She scratched her head and stifled a yawn. "No, but I sort of know her through the queer nightlife scene, and her girlfriend is the bassist for The Fiery Ones."

He laughed. "Man, that band sucks. How are they so popular?"

"Every town needs their pretentious scremo band, Oliver. Don't hold it against them. They're giving the people what they think they want."

He cleared his throat. "True. Okay, back to business. Be at the QROK studio at eleven thirty. They won't need you to play, just chat with Kelli. Call me afterward."

"Capiche. Later."

She laid back on the bed again. Her thoughts turned to Maddy's text. She opened the message again and texted a reply. *Good morning to you too. So, I guess I'm going to be on the radio today. QROK at noon.*

Seconds later, she got a response.

That's so cool! I'm going to put it on while the guys and I prep for tonight. Then I can brag about you. :)

She blushed at the thought of Maddy talking about her to the cooks and kitchen staff.

Now I'm blushing.

Perfect, exactly the response I was hoping for. Good luck today.

She closed her eyes and reveled in the reciprocity of her… whatever this was…with Maddy. No chasing. No awkward moments. It just felt amazing and so right. Just then she heard a distant scream coming from the kitchen. She sat up with a start.

"Coming, buddy!" She hurried down the hallway to scoop out a fishy peace offering to Eddie.

CHAPTER EIGHTEEN

The air conditioning was blasting at the QROK studio while Nat sat in the waiting room for Kelli K. The décor was an attempt to be effortlessly hip, but as the daughter of a designer, she could see how desperately hard they were trying. Ripped leather couches that cost over five grand each and came pre-torn. Minimalist art that felt too small for the large black and white walls. A PBR vending machine. Oh, the humanity! QROK had once been one of New York's greatest rock stations, but over time it was bought and sold and was now a shadow of its former self. Still, lots of great artists appeared on air to promote albums and tours.

Nat wasn't above a little hustle. In fact, it was her hustle that got her song on *Trauma University* in the first place. Back before she had her apartment and sold out shows, she was trying to make it in the big city just like everyone else. A friend of a friend told her who the music producer would be for the new show, and she sussed out where the producer hung out, and Nat booked gigs on multiple nights there, hoping to catch her eye.

Apparently, it worked. The hustle was hard but was often worth it.

"Nat Chambers! It's wonderful to see you!" A woman resembling a hipsterfied version of Taylor Swift stood with bangled fists on her leather miniskirt.

She stood and held out her hand. "Great to see you again, Kelli."

"Look at you, so formal. We've got to loosen you up before the show. Would you like a beer?" she asked, motioning to the PBR machine.

"Ah, no thanks. I'll just have some water."

She waved her hand, beckoning Nat to follow her. "Come. Let's get you all set up and comfy in the studio, shall we?"

The studio itself was like every other studio out there, which Nat found comforting. Black foam adorned the walls to dampen the sound, microphones swung on metal arms, headsets that were usually beyond stretched out so that they wouldn't pinch your ears.

Nat settled in and got suited up while Kelli flitted about, doing vocal exercises and head rolls.

"Thirty seconds, ladies," the sound engineer said through the room mic. Kelli took her place and leaned in to Nat.

"We're just going to chit chat about your tour, your upcoming album, all that fun stuff. Maybe a little gossip, too."

Nat smiled uneasily. "Ah, gossip isn't really my thing."

Kelli gave her a wink. "Well, it's my thing, darling."

Before she could protest any further, she heard the engineer break in their headsets with the three-second countdown. Then theme music filled her ears and Kelli pounced on the mic. "Hey there New York, how the hell are you? It's a beautiful day in the city. You can barely smell the garbage. That's a miracle. Today we have a very special guest. Fans of *Trauma University* will know her as the singer/songwriter behind the show's stellar theme song. She's also hotter than the subway in August, if I do say so myself. I'm so pleased to have Nat Chambers in the studio. Hi Nat!"

She leaned in to her mic. "Hi Kelli, thanks for having me."

"I can't believe we managed to get you in town, Nat. It seems like you're always touring these days."

"Yeah, well it's really important for indie musicians to put themselves out there and tour," she answered honestly. "I mean, it's tough to make a living off record sales since no one really buys records anymore. They stream."

"Don't I know it. Come on people! You love a song on the radio, support the album, right?" It was obvious that this was something important to Kelli as well, as most of her circle were working musicians.

Nat continued. "Don't get me wrong. I totally get it. And while that's a wonderful way to get your music out there, it doesn't necessarily translate to something you can live on as an artist. You're looking at maybe a hundred bucks per a hundred thousand plays."

"Unreal."

"So yes, touring is still super important, and I love getting to meet people who like listening to my music."

"I'm pretty sure those are called fans, Nat." Kelli raised her eyebrow.

She blushed. "I don't really like to think of it that way. We're all in this together. We all have skills, something to give to one another. That's just what I do. I get the chance to ignite something in someone else. I don't take that for granted."

"Good looking and humble, too. It's really too much, Nat."

She laughed. "Okay, now you're embarrassing me. But thank you."

"So, since you are always on the road, what do you have planned next?"

"The band is hitting Philadelphia in a few weeks and then we're off to Europe for a bit. Then the plan is to get back in the studio and record the new album."

"Have you got all kinds of new goodies to share with your fans? I mean, your fellow humans?" Kelli rolled her eyes in a teasing way.

Lie. Lie, stupid. She had started a few things but she was far from having an album's worth of material. "Uh, it's coming along," she said with a smile she hoped was convincing.

Kelli shifted in her seat and leaned closer to her mic. "Well, as much as I love talking about touring and new albums, I actually want to ask you about your last big tour with Melissa Hartford."

It felt like the room suddenly became very warm, and she could feel pinpricks of sweat form on her forehead. This was the absolute last thing she wanted to talk about. "Ah yeah, the Nat Chambers Band has actually been touring since then. We have an amazing new addition, Jackie Adeyemi, who slays the cello, and of course, my right-hand man Paul Lim is still drumming away."

"Of course! Jackie and Paul are wonderful. But the tour you did with Melissa was a big deal. I hear people still talk about it all the time. Ever plan on touring with her again?"

Was Kelli working for Melissa's manager? How the hell could Nat answer this diplomatically? Her throat went dry and she took a quick swig from her water bottle.

"I'm really just focused on making music with Paul and Jackie right now," she said. *Good answer. Oliver would approve.*

There was a flicker, however, in Kelli's eyes, and Nat could feel the small studio closing in around her.

"So, rumor is you and Melissa had a little thing going on."

Kelli's words were like a bomb going off in her brain, sending any cohesive thoughts blasting in all directions and worst of all, Maddy would be listening to the show. They had never discussed Nat's relationship with Melissa. This was not the way she wanted Maddy or the world to find out about her massive lapse in judgement.

She collected herself and attempted to do some damage control. "Melissa and I worked very well together on that tour and it was a very successful collaboration." At this point, she was practically glaring at Kelli, but it didn't seem to faze the host.

"Ah come on, that's not what I asked you. Give our listeners a little hot gossip. Are the rumors true? Cuz sweetie, I saw you guys perform together and it was practically foreplay."

She wondered if there was a way she could will herself to spontaneously combust to escape this torture. Kelli was purposely ignoring her body language and there were few ways out of this conversation that made anyone look good.

"Listen," she said, as she squeezed the bridge of her nose. "I've never made any attempt to hide who I am. Everyone who knows me knows I'm queer. I'm proud of that. I'm over the moon that some gay kid in rural Iowa can listen to my songs and know that I'm singing about another woman, and if that makes them feel even a tiny bit less alone, then it's all worth it. I will talk for days about how very gay I am, but I also want to keep my private life exactly that, private. Maybe one day that will change, but right here and right now, I'm not taking the bait, Kelli." She gritted her teeth but said it all with a smile.

Kelli's face told Nat she'd won this little battle. "Nat Chambers will be keeping us all in suspense then?"

"I guess so, Kelli."

"Well thank you for being here Nat! It's about time to switch things over to our commercial free block. Speaking of blocks, here's the Nat Chambers Band with 'Heart/Block' to kick us off." With that, Kelli pulled off her headphones and avoided eye contact.

Nat took her headset off and stood. "What the hell was that? You totally ambushed me."

She sighed with exasperation. "Come on Nat! Everyone in Brooklyn knows that you and Melissa were screwing all through that tour. You may want to keep your private life private, but Melissa sure doesn't. She confirmed it to me over drinks a few weeks back."

Nat was speechless.

Kelli tilted her head to the side, in an almost sympathetic movement. "Listen, I'm sorry if it came as a shock. I do have a fanbase to appeal to and ratings to make. If it's any consolation, Melissa is still really hung up on you."

She pursed her lips and headed for the door. "You know, weirdly enough, it's not at all. Good luck with your ratings." With that, she pulled the door shut tightly behind her and stormed out of the station.

When she hit the street, she pulled out her phone and saw about a dozen frantic texts from Oliver. She dialed his number.

"Nat, I had no idea she was going to pull that shit on you."

After being cooped up in that room, she could finally breathe. "I know, Ollie. You would have never let that happen. Turns out she's friends with Melissa and I was easy pickings for some ratings."

"Her studio manager is going to get an earful from me," he said, his tough guy persona peeking through.

"Just forget it. It will just make things worse. I really want to put all that behind me, ok?"

He huffed into the phone. "If that's what you want, you got it. But Kelli K is on my shit list from now on."

She smiled. "Thanks. Talk to you later."

She headed toward the coffee shop on the corner. An iced coffee with lots of sugar would help her pull herself together. As she made it inside, her phone buzzed in her hand. It was a message from Maddy. Shit. Shit shit shit. She was listening and now she's going to be hurt or pissed. Nat winced as she opened the message.

You were awesome today. My assistant George won't stop singing "Heart/Block." If you aren't busy tomorrow, would you want to come help me make some pastries?

She was perplexed. Did Maddy hear the same interview? She wasn't going to look a gift horse in the mouth if she escaped this one unscathed. *I'd love to. What time?*

Is nine okay? I know musicians aren't exactly early risers.

Hey, some of us actually do wake up before noon. I'll see you then.

She would need to set an alarm. Who was she kidding? Years of staying up late and playing gigs had conditioned her to be a night owl, not that she was going to admit that to Maddy right now. She hadn't mucked things up completely, and that was good because she really liked her. They hadn't had sex yet, but Nat was over the moon. The barista gave her a mumbled hello.

"I'll take a large iced coffee with two sugars. Sorry, four sugars."

CHAPTER NINETEEN

Nat brushed imperceivable cat hair from her jeans and did a quick sweep of her ponytail to make sure it was still the smooth miracle she had spent a good hour trying to achieve. Normally she abhorred ponytails. What was the point of having long hair if you couldn't let it run wild? Maddy's collection of braids and ponytails however had managed to win Nat's heart. Plus, she figured if she was going to be in a professional kitchen, she should at least try to keep any unpleasant surprises out Touché's dessert course.

She knocked firmly on the kitchen door and moments later was greeted by a rather stout man with a salt and pepper goatee, wearing a chef's coat. He looked at her for a moment before grinning broadly and surprisingly bursting into song.

"Heart/block, you got me begging for your sweet talk," he sang with a heavy accent but pleasantly on pitch.

She couldn't help but laugh. "You must be George." She reached out her hand. He took it in his meaty paw and shook it heartily.

"Come in! Chef is just finishing up a call," he said.

He led her through what she imagined was the most pristine kitchen in New York City. White tiles gleamed. Knives were hung with care on magnetic strips. The stainless steel that filled the kitchen was polished and buffed.

She turned to him. "This place is so clean. Does anyone actually do any cooking here?"

He gave her another smirk. "Wait until dinner at eight o'clock. It'll look like a middle school cafeteria food fight." He nodded in the direction of a small office. "Here she comes."

Maddy walked out dressed in her chef whites with her red hair tied in a tight braid. Nat didn't realize she had a thing for women in uniforms until just that moment. Maddy smiled so big and brightly it colored her cheeks with crimson.

"Hi, you," Nat said.

"Hi, yourself." Maddy glanced over at George. "George, thank you so much for letting Nat in. Did he sing for you? He promised that he would."

"Oh, he did and it was epic."

He smiled and waved to the women as he walked off into another part of the kitchen.

Maddy squeezed her hand. "Come, I'll show you my office." She pulled her gently down the hall and into a room with not much more than a small desk, a laptop and a few papers.

"So, this is where the…clerical magic happens?" she asked as Maddy gently closed the door behind them.

Nat could see Maddy was focused on her lips and didn't answer. Well, with words at least. Maddy backed her up against the door and kissed her passionately. She returned the gesture, wrapping her arms around Maddy's waist and pulling Maddy tightly against her. Maddy's lips were soft and sweet as she traced her tongue against them. The scent of oranges filled the air around them and only added to the heady moment.

Maddy pulled away from the kiss and placed her head against Nat's neck. "Okay, I know this is super unprofessional, but I just had to touch you for a moment," she said breathlessly, as if she'd been running a marathon.

"Uh huh," Nat managed to get out. Her jeans were now damp with desire and she was pretty sure her perfect ponytail had gone to shit.

Maddy ran her fingers along Nat's jaw. "I didn't ask you here to do that, I swear. I really do want you to hang out and make things with me today. I just…" Maddy nipped at her chin and they began kissing again. She thought she was going to burst but as each kiss flew by, she mercifully remained intact. Ridiculously turned on and high on the scent of oranges, but intact.

Maddy pulled away again, this time putting some physical distance between them. "Phew, okay. We need to get out there before the guys think we're getting it on in here. I shit you not, they'll be lined up with a glass at the door," she said with a laugh.

"Whatever you say, Chef." Nat was pâte à choux in Maddy's hands.

Maddy bit her bottom lip. "That was kind of hot when you called me chef. Come on, let's get you an apron."

She followed Maddy to a wire rack where they retrieved a long, white apron and Maddy leaned in and tied it neatly around her waist.

Nat brushed her nose against Maddy's neck. "So, Chef, why do you smell like the world's sexiest orange grove?"

Maddy threw her head back and laughed. "I was making dark chocolate and orange tarts with smoked Cointreau caviar and I spilled the Cointreau all over me."

"If it tastes anything like it smells, then you deserve a James Beard Award."

Maddy cocked her eyebrow. "Would you like to try it? It's a new recipe."

Her eyes opened wide. "Yes, please."

"Come on back to my work station. It's chilling in the walk-in."

She followed Maddy to another clean white area of the kitchen with a large stainless-steel table in the middle. Maddy popped into the walk-in and emerged a moment later with the shiniest, most decadent looking tart Nat had ever seen. There were small orange pearls on top of the almost black ganache, and the scent of toasted wood and orange trees teased her senses.

"Maddy, it's so beautiful. I can see my reflection in it."

"Then it is definitely beautiful." Maddy winked at her. "Here." Maddy cut into the tart with a fork and revealed its velvety inside. She raised the fork to her lips. As the tart hit her tongue, she was filled with fragments of memories: the salty spray of the beach where she would spend vacations as a teenager. The sensual bitterness of her first taste of dark chocolate. The vibrant, sweet acidity of the fresh squeezed orange juice her grandmother used to make during their visits to Brazil in the summers before she passed away. What Maddy could do was masterful, and it wasn't just talent. She was an artist.

"Well?"

She didn't even realize she's been lost in a daze since she took a bite. "It's like you tapped into my own happy memories. It wasn't just a taste; it was an experience."

Maddy's eyes blinked away tears and Nat panicked. "Oh no. Did I say something wrong? I meant it as a compliment."

Maddy shook her head as she blinked away a tear. "No. That's everything I've ever wanted to hear. This all means so much to me. I'm just…touched, I guess."

"Well, I am too. Thank you for sharing this with me. Is this what we're making today because I'm a little terrified I might ruin it."

Maddy chuckled. "No, sweetie, don't worry." *Sweetie.* "We're making lemon almond scones for the Senior Gay and Lesbian Center's bridge tournament this afternoon."

"Are you serious?"

"Absolutely. I try to make something yummy for them once a week. Touché's owner is a big supporter, so he lets me use our supplies and space to do it."

Nat steadied herself on the steel prep table. Did she just actually swoon? "The more I learn about you, Maddy, the more I want to know."

"Then go wash your hands and grab that container of flour over there and I'll tell you anything you want."

She did so and watched as Maddy glided around the prep area, touching her anytime she slid by to grab the butter or baking soda.

"Okay, can you measure me out three cups of leveled flour? Then a half cup of sugar, a teaspoon of salt, and a tablespoon of baking powder?"

She nodded and went to work. "So why New York? You loved Paris."

"New York is the city of new experience and taking risks," she replied as she sliced sticks of butter into cubes. "I learned the techniques in Paris, but I wanted to do something different. I needed the space to be creative. I got that by working in restaurants and bakeries here, and at Touché I'm given a lot of freedom." She added the butter to Nat's bowl. "You know, it's not even really about freedom. I just want to be understood. I lived so much of my life feeling like nobody got me, that it's just really important to me now. Does that make sense?"

"Absolutely. I think that's why Paul and I have been playing together for so long. He just gets me; he always has. Jackie is newer but it's the same with her. We all just have this unspoken language, and I think that's what makes us a good band."

Maddy opened a drawer and pulled out a tool Nat had never seen before and started cutting the butter into the flour. "I think that's really clear when you see the three of you together. You seem like a family."

"We are. Totally. We do a lot together. Go to shows, celebrate holidays, create, go to museums. We love to devour the city together."

Maddy's strong forearm muscles twitched as she mixed the dough together and Nat couldn't help but stare.

"Promise not to judge me, but I haven't done much of that since moving here."

"What?"

"Explore. I've been so focused on building my career, I honestly haven't had much time for museums or Broadway or…well, much of anything. In fact, you are only the second person I've dated since moving to the city, and the first one was so casual that I didn't really mind when she stopped texting. I don't think we went on a proper date. Do people even do that anymore? Can you pass me a half a cup of milk?"

She measured the liquid out and passed it to Maddy.

"How are you with zesting?"

"The zestiest. All yellow, no white, right?"

Maddy smiled. "You got it." She handed a lemon to Nat.

Nat suddenly felt bold. "So, you and me... It's more than casual to you?"

Maddy stopped mixing the dough and stepped toward her. "Oh, Natalia." She kissed Nat lightly on the lips, then the nose, and chin. "I am very serious about this."

Nat murmured with pleasure at Maddy's words and the feather-lightness of her kisses. She took Maddy's flour-covered hand in hers and whispered, "I want you. So much."

"Oh god, Natalia, what you do to me," Maddy whispered, her lips close to Nat's ear. "I'm so wet right now." The kitchen began to swim as Nat leaned in to kiss Maddy's neck.

"Hey, Chef!" a voice called. George popped his head around the corner to see them standing too close to be doing any constructive baking. "Uh, Chef, sorry to interrupt. Was just checking when you wanted those scones to be delivered to the center."

Maddy cleared her throat. "Uh, about forty-five minutes will be perfect. Thank you, George." He chuckled and disappeared. Maddy laughed nervously.

"Do you think he noticed?" Nat asked.

"Please. Those guys have been rooting for this since you stopped in that first night. Anyway, we should probably finish these scones."

"Yes, scones. That's all I will think about from now on. Tender, sweet, kissable, sexy scones."

"I love that you don't take yourself too seriously," Maddy said. "It seems like everyone in the city does, but you don't. Why?"

She had never really thought about it. "I guess I just want to get through the day and have a little bit to smile about when my head hits the pillow. I used to take things too close to heart, but when you put aside all the bullshit, we're all just people and no one is any more important than anyone else."

Maddy grinned simply. "I like your philosophy. Can you reach those sliced almonds? You have a couple inches on me."

She reached up on her tip toes and grabbed the almonds from the top shelf.

Maddy pulled out a pan and turned on the burner behind them. "The trick to toasting nuts is to stop when you start to smell them. Can you squeeze those lemons for me?" Maddy turned her back, while Nat dutifully squeezed away. "So, you and Melissa Hartford, huh?" She winced. At least she didn't have to make eye contact right now.

"Yeah," she sighed. "Me and Melissa Hartford. It didn't last long and it was really messy. I probably should've told you, but it was over months before I even met you." Lemon juice splashed on her hands, seeping into a small cut and adding a sense of stinging drama to the whole conversation.

"Nat, it's fine," Maddy replied as she tossed the nuts in the pan. "I mean, I would've liked to hear it from you personally, but you don't owe me a synopsis of your dating life. I guess I got weirdly jealous. She's like this big-deal musician. You must have a special connection."

The fragrant smell of almonds drifted toward Nat. "Well, there's no need to be jealous. I even turned down another tour with her. I lost a best friend and my dignity to Melissa, and I don't need to give her another moment of my time."

Maddy turned and looked at Nat. Her eyes were soft and warm. "Okay, so no Melissa talk."

Nat nodded. "No Melissa talk. I much prefer talking about Madeline."

"I hear she makes a mean scone."

"You don't even know the half of it. She's smart and sexy and I can't stop thinking about her."

Maddy licked her lips. "Come here."

Nat followed her request until they were just an inch apart.

"My almonds are toasted," Maddy said breathlessly, holding back a laugh.

"And hilarious. Did I mention she's hilarious?"

They made quick work of the scones, rolling out the dough and cutting them into the classic triangle shapes. While they baked, Maddy introduced Nat to the rest of the kitchen crew, who all robustly serenaded her with a few lines from "Heart/ Block" as well. Maddy showed her around the restaurant, they snuck a chilly kiss in the walk-in, and sampled some of the evening's wines.

"Mmm, this one will be perfect with the Cointreau tart," Maddy declared as she sipped on a red zin from Napa. She passed the glass to Nat, who had to agree. It would be wonderful with the bitter chocolate and citrus.

"How do you come up with your ideas?" Nat asked as they sat close together at Touché's reclaimed wood bar.

"I really love classic flavors, but with a twist. I fell in love with molecular gastronomy, so I play around with that as much as I can without completely alienating our guests," she laughed. "I mean, I don't want someone to be so turned off by technique that they lose the essence of what I'm trying to bring them."

"And what is it that you are trying to bring them?"

"A memory. A feeling. A fleeting moment that passes through their taste buds and speaks to their hearts. God, it sounds so pretentious when I say it like that, but I mean it. I want to feed people's souls, not just their stomachs. Pastry—baking—saved me. It gave me purpose. It's like a religion to me."

"I don't think it sounds pretentious at all," Nat said as she rubbed her thumb along Maddy's hand. "I think it sounds beautiful."

"Chef, your scones are done," George called from behind the swinging kitchen door.

"Oh shit, we better grab them before they burn!"

Maddy leapt up and Nat was close behind her. The scones were safe. George had carefully removed them from the oven when they were golden brown and gorgeous and placed them in the cooling rack.

"You're a saint, George!" Maddy called.

"*Sí, lo sé,*" he shouted from the other side of the kitchen.

"So, shall we glaze?" Maddy asked.

"Let's get our glaze on."

Maddy combined lemon juice, a small amount of zest, milk, vanilla and powdered sugar until it became smooth and glossy. "Want to do the honors?"

"No, please. I'll be the almond-placer-on-er."

"Deal."

Maddy dipped the warm scones in the bright lemony glaze and placed them on a tray where Nat affixed perfectly toasted almond slices. She had to admit, they looked mighty fine.

"The senior center is going to have the most rocking bridge party ever with these scones," Nat declared.

Maddy laughed. "You would know, my rock star. I mean, rock star person. Ugh, sorry, getting a little ahead of myself." She blushed.

"I'll be your rock star if you want," she said sweetly.

"I'd like that."

"I should probably get going and let you finish your prep. Thank you for letting me help you today. Honestly, we could have been making dog biscuits and I would have been happy just to be here with you."

"I do have a great recipe for those."

"I bet you do. Can I kiss you goodbye?"

"Please do."

She took Maddy by the apron and kissed her. "When can I see you again?"

"I'm free on Monday. All day."

"Then I'll see you soon."

Nat woke up the next day with Maddy on her mind and Eddie sitting on her head. While he purred away, she thought about their searing kisses and how Maddy made her head spin just by standing near her.

As she practiced songs for the tour and tidied up her apartment, she knew she wanted to do something epic for Maddy and take her on a date she'd never forget. She'd need some assistance though, so she sent an SOS text to Paul and Jackie, asking them to meet at her apartment as soon as possible.

An hour later the bandmates showed up. Jackie was freshly showered and Paul was scruffy and sipping on an iced coffee. He plopped himself on the couch while Jackie practically floated into an armchair.

"What's the situation, Chambers?" Paul asked, his voice gruff from an obvious late night.

"Okay, so… I need to plan the perfect date," she declared as she smiled hopefully at them.

Jackie and Paul looked at each other, then at Nat.

"Seriously, Chambers?" Paul asked. "You woke me up for that?"

"Well, it's two in the afternoon…" Nat remarked.

"Aw, I think it's adorable. She's helpless Paul, like a baby bird. A horny, gay baby bird," cooed Jackie.

"It's not about being horny! Okay, it's a little about being horny, but Maddy is like… She's special." Nat looked at her friends, imploring them to help her.

"Well, shit. Now you've tugged at my heartstrings." Paul cleared his throat and then cracked his knuckles. "Okay first of all, Jackie…get a pen and some paper. Nat, order pizza, extra pepperoni. I need nourishment if I'm going to be on top of my game. Operation Seal the Deal is now in effect."

After a few hours of pizza, planning, and phone calls, Paul and Jackie headed home, leaving Nat to text Maddy and officially invite her out. Nat kept her plans close to the vest but told Maddy she'd be there to pick her up at eleven a.m. When Nat went to bed that night, it took a good hour for the butterflies in her stomach to join her in slumber.

CHAPTER TWENTY

The next morning, Nat's hands were sweaty as she fiddled with the air conditioning in the back of the black car.

"Eh, you want it the Arctic in here or what?" asked Gino, her driver, in his gruff but not unkind voice.

"Sorry, Gino. I'm weirdly nervous. Is it too much? Do you think it's too much? I mean if you were a girl…well, a woman, a lady, would this be too much?"

He laughed and sucked his teeth. "Well, if I were a lady, I think I'd be impressed. But then again I've always had a flair for the dramatic."

They pulled in front of Maddy's building and Nat shot off a text that she was outside. Moments later Maddy bounded down the steps, her hair down, dusting her shoulders. Nat swallowed hard. Maddy was wearing a short but flowy dress dotted with green and yellow flowers, and a denim jacket. She looked stunning. Nat hopped out of the car to greet her, and Maddy practically leapt into her embrace.

"Hi," Nat said, her cheeks flushed with excitement and desire.

"Hi yourself," Maddy replied, taking a piece of Nat's hair and twirling it in her slender fingers. Maddy gestured to the car. "What's this?"

She cleared her throat. "Well, this right here is the best black car service in all of Manhattan and our ride for the day."

"Oh, that's so nice! The subway is particularly ripe this week, so you get major points for this, Natalia Chambers."

She slid in beside Maddy. Their legs brushed up against each other, and even through her jeans she could feel the electricity between them.

"Maddy, this is Gino. Gino, the lovely Madeline." She gestured to the bulky figure behind the glass partition.

"Hello, lovely Madeline," he said, making sure to emphasize all the syllables in the way that only Italian New Yorkers can.

Maddy smiled widely. "Hi, Gino."

Nat reached over and grabbed a to-go mug of hot chocolate and small paper box and handed it to her.

"What's this?"

She tucked a strand of her hair behind her ear. "Well, you are not the only person who knows how to use le Google. Open it."

She cracked open the box to discover a flakey surprise. "Is this a DKA from Dominique Ansel?"

"Yup. I read that feature in *New York Magazine*'s 'Thirty Chefs Under Thirty,' and you said it was your favorite pastry that you didn't make yourself."

"It is! How did you get this, though? That line is like three hours long."

"Oh, I got there at seven a.m.," she said, taking an exaggerated sip of her latte.

Gino made an "ahem" noise from the front seat.

"Okay, *we* got there at seven a.m. In all fairness, Gino, you sat in the car and did not have to witness the epic battle between a rat and a pigeon over a slice of pizza."

"I miss all da good stuff."

"Well, I am very touched and super impressed, Nat. I don't think anyone has ever waited in line for pastry for me," Maddy giggled.

"Well hold on to it because we are moving on to our first location. Gino, let's get our Central Park on."

As he put the car into drive, Maddy reached over and took her hand. The car seemed to fly up Broadway, and before long they were at the eastern entrance to the park. The women got out of the car, and he popped the trunk to reveal a picnic basket and plush blankets, which Nat scooped up in her arms. They walked along the pathway to the lush East Green, where there was plenty of space to spread out underneath a nearby black cherry tree. Nat laid down the blankets and offered her hand to Maddy.

"You know, I don't think I've ever done this," Maddy said, smoothing her skirt as she settled in.

"Really?" Nat asked as she unpacked the basket's selection of fruits and cheeses.

"Yeah, I guess I was just so focused on my work—ooh Humboldt Fog cheese, nice—that I kind of forgot to experience the city as much as I could."

"Well, today you are going to experience the hell out of New York."

She reached over and tugged on the hem of Nat's T-shirt. "Come here."

Nat leaned over and Maddy took her face in her hands and kissed her long and slow. When Nat pulled away, Maddy's eyes were still closed.

"You make my head spin, Natalia."

"And I am nothing but butterflies whenever you're around, Madeline. I can barely form sentences. My tongue is tied."

"Is that so? Let me see." Maddy pulled her in for another kiss, this time deeper and more urgent. "Hmm, works just fine from this perspective." Maddy purred. Nat couldn't help but laugh, which in turn made Maddy laugh.

"That. That was cheesier than this Humboldt Fog."

"God, I know."

"I loved it." Nat gazed at Maddy's face. Her eyes seemed to change between green and light brown by the second. The sprinkle of freckles across her nose and cheeks. The way she bit her lip when she was thinking of what to say. Whatever was happening here was special and filled Nat with a warmth and giddiness she hadn't felt in…well, she couldn't remember when. Maybe never.

"Okay, speaking of that Humboldt Fog," Maddy said, breaking Nat from her dreamlike state, "pass that over here."

"I admit, I'm not the most well-versed in cheeses, but the woman at the shop said it went well with figs, so I got some of those too." She pulled out a small basket of ripe figs and presented them to Maddy.

"God. I love figs," Maddy squeaked as she palmed one and raised it to her nose. "What about you?"

She scratched her cheek. "Do Fig Newtons count? I have actually never had a fig all on its own."

Maddy sat up on her knees. "What? Are you serious? Well, you are in for a treat. Close your eyes."

Nat opened her mouth as Maddy placed the delicate, sweet flesh on her tongue. She bit down and soon the fruit's honey-like liqueur filled her mouth. It was tender and crunchy at the same time. She chewed and savored it, and when she opened her eyes, Maddy was looking back at her with hunger.

"Wow, watching you eat that, I am super-hot right now."

"Join the club, Chef."

Maddy ran her finger along Nat's chin, gathering a pearl of fig juice that had settled there. She licked it and Nat moaned softly. "Okay, okay. I think we need a time-out because I really, really want you."

"Mmm."

"And as much as I want you, I want to give you an experience in the city. I want to know you. Tell me everything and let me watch you eat your cronut." Nat slid the paper box over.

Maddy laughed. "It's not a cronut. I'm not a tourist from Ohio. It's different. It's more refined."

"Pardon me, I stand corrected." She reached into the picnic basket and pulled out a bottle of wine and two small jam jars. "Oh, would you like some rosé to go along with your 'not cronut'?"

"I thought you'd never ask."

They sat and told stories about their first kisses (disastrous) and falling in love with their careers (lifesaving). Once they had their fill of cheese and pastry, Nat sat up on her knees. "So, are you ready for the next adventure?"

Maddy rose to her knees as well. "Always. Where are we heading?"

"To meet some dinosaurs."

CHAPTER TWENTY-ONE

"You are full of surprises, Natalia," Maddy said as they stood at the bottom of the steps of the American Museum of Natural History.

Nat smiled and took Maddy's hand. They ran up the steps like little kids, giggling the whole way. They stopped at the information desk, where a surly looking, elderly volunteer stood.

"Excuse me, madam, could you please direct us to your finest dinosaurs?" Nat asked, while Maddy covered a smile with her hand.

The old woman was not amused. "The Hall of Fossils is on the fourth floor."

She handed Nat a map but Nat politely declined. "You see, we are having an adventure, and adventure needs no map, except for maybe the women's restroom. We had some wine with lunch."

The volunteer just stared.

"Thank you!" Nat shouted over her shoulder as they headed toward the stairs.

Their heels clicked against the marble floors and the laughter of little kids echoed off the tall ceilings. She couldn't help but be nostalgic, remembering when her parents would make the annual trip with her to the city and let her take in these massive beasts. They stood in front of a fearsome T-Rex and Maddy gave her hand a squeeze.

"Everyone is always so impressed by the T-Rex, but I have to say I think it's overrated," Nat said. "I mean, sure, those teeth, but also, those arms. What a cosmic joke."

"When I was growing up, we were taught that man and dinosaurs walked the earth at the same time," Maddy added, staring up at the fossil and then turning to meet Nat's gaze. "Evangelical upbringing. Imagine my surprise when I learned about evolution in my late teens. All that time I thought going out to gather berries meant becoming a potential dinosaur snack."

Nat tried to hide a laugh. "I'm sorry."

"Go ahead. I found *Jurassic Park* to be a very confusing experience."

Nat wrapped her arm around Maddy's waist. "Thank god for Laura Dern."

"Ohhh, you had a crush on her too?"

"I'm pretty sure I'm a lesbian because of Laura Dern."

"Aren't we all? Thank heavens for the Dernissance. Okay, well since you think the T-Rex is overrated, which dinosaur is your favorite?"

Nat tilted her head and motioned for Maddy to follow. They stopped in front of the large Apatosaurus on display.

"Look at this goober," Nat said, motioning to the long and spiny skeleton. "Tiny head, huge body. Vegan. I mean, what more could you ask for? Plus, the best part is that for years the museum had the wrong head on this thing."

"That must have been awkward for her," Maddy said, a hint of sympathy in her voice.

They continued through the exhibits and then found a secluded bench to rest for a moment.

"So, you grew up evangelical. What was that like?" Nat asked while pushing a lock of curls out of Maddy's beautiful face.

"Weird. Wonderful. Confusing. Equal amount of shame and love," Maddy responded. "My mom died when I was seven, and before that, we were just casual churchgoers. After her death, though, my dad really threw himself into the church. I guess he needed something to believe in.

"It wasn't always bad with him. When I was young, he did his best. He thought spending our free time in church would help, and in ways it did. There were a lot of wonderful people who helped raise me. But as I got older, I became curious about the big world outside the tiny one my dad had built for me. I had a terrible crush on my bible camp counselor when I was twelve. When I came home, it was pretty obvious I was infatuated with her, and my father wanted to put an end to that immediately. "

"So, what happened?" Nat asked.

"Well, no more bible camp or other female role models, that was for sure. I quickly learned to hide those feelings away and only allowed myself to feel them in my most quiet moments."

"But at some point, that no longer worked?"

"Exactly. My feelings for my first girlfriend Chelsea were too big to completely hide away. My body reacted when she walked in a room. My mind was so full of thoughts of her and what it felt like to be alive in that way, I got careless. That's when my dad figured it all out. Also, small towns aren't so great for keeping secrets."

Nat took Maddy's hand in hers and lifted it to her lips. "So now there are no more secrets."

Maddy smiled as Nat kissed her hand then her wrist. "Yeah, fuck secrets."

"How long has it been now since you last spoke to your dad?"

The smile dropped from Maddy's face. She cleared her throat. "Seven years. Do you mind if we talk about something else?"

"Of course not. I'm sorry."

"No." Maddy caressed Nat's cheeks. "It's good that you care. I want you to know me. I'm just having such an amazing time that I don't want to think about that right now. I want to think about your warm cheeks and the way you smell like leather and cardamom."

"Is that a good thing?"

"Oh yes, a very good thing."

Nat leaned in and kissed Maddy. It was getting harder and harder to resist her lips, her hips, and everything else Maddy related.

"Wow, okay, so we have one more place to go," Nat declared, a little too loudly.

Maddy licked her lips and hooked her finger on the edge of Nat's T-shirt collar. "Yeah?"

"Yeah. Ahem, uh, let me text Gino and tell him to pick us up." She took a deep breath in and blew it out slowly. Maddy's skirt exposed her strong and lean legs, and it took everything in Nat to look away. They held hands in silence and made their way to Gino's car.

"What, no present? I was hoping for one of them dino heads on a stick," Gino said as they slid across the leather seats.

"Next time, I promise," Nat said. "So, here's where we are going next." She handed him a slip of paper.

"You got it."

"Where are we headed?"

"Oh, it's a surprise."

"You are a woman of endless mystery."

Nat simply smiled and tried to think of anything besides running her hands along Maddy's bare legs. Twenty of the longest minutes passed, and they reached their destination: a brick building in the heart of Alphabet City.

"Here we are," Nat announced. "See you later, Gino."

They stepped out of the car and up to a rusty metal door. Nat rang a button and soon the sound of a buzzer charged the air around them. She gently took Maddy's hand and led her down a dark hallway and up a set of stairs. She knocked on a door that was painted black like the rest of the walls. A moment later, it swung open.

"Maddy, this is Hollis. They are the proprietor of this magical little place."

Hollis was a stunning figure with a shock of blue hair and colorful tattoos decorating their arms. Nat greeted them with a quick kiss on the cheek.

"Nice to meet you, Hollis." Maddy reached out her hand and Hollis took it and placed a small kiss on it.

"A pleasure," Hollis responded, their voice warm and soft. They turned to Nat.

"Everything is ready for you, old friend."

"I can't thank you enough, Hollis," Nat gushed. Hollis motioned them inside and led them down another hallway lit with small, round floor lights. They pushed back a set of black curtains, and inside was a small, classic movie theatre. Ornate art deco sconces hung from the walls. The chairs were velvet and plush, a deep red burst of nostalgia. The scent of popcorn hung in the air, and in the middle of the section, waiting for them, was a bucket of the fluffy stuff and two glasses of champagne.

"Oh Natalia, it's like a dream," Maddy said, as she looked around in awe.

"Hollis has one of the best hidden gems in New York. They have been collecting these authentic pieces for years, and they only show movies on a projector." Nat took Maddy's hand again and led her to their seats.

As soon as they settled in, the lights dimmed and the screen lit up a ghostly white. Nat raised her glass of champagne. "To you for spending the day with me and trusting me with this adventure."

Maddy lifted her glass in response. "To you and the best date of my life."

They clinked glasses and took a sip as the film began to roll.

Maddy looked up at the screen and gasped. "Oh my god, is this *The Umbrellas of Cherbourg*?"

"Yes. I asked Hollis for a classic French film, and they promised this would be a hit."

"It's one of my favorites," Maddy confessed, bringing a huge smile to both their faces. Maddy leaned over and kissed her slowly. She could taste the champagne on the tip of her tongue, and the hair on the back of her neck began to rise. She broke the kiss, however, as much as she didn't want to, motioning to the screen. Maddy smiled contently, and leaned her shoulder into Nat, interlacing their fingers.

Throughout the movie, they ignored their popcorn, choosing to use their hands instead to caress knees, thighs, and the insides of delicate forearms. It was exquisite torture for Nat, whose arousal rose to a fever pitch. As the credits rolled, her skin was flush and her heart was in her throat.

"I want you to take me home," Maddy said softly, breaking their silence. Nat looked at her, disappointment creeping in.

"Oh, sure, of course. I can have Gino drop you off—"

"No." Maddy put her fingers to Nat's mouth and pressed her mouth against Nat's ear. "I want you to take me to *your* place."

Nat felt a shock of desire pulse in her. She led her out of the space and into the waiting car. As they slid in, Maddy took Nat's face in her hands and hungrily kissed her mouth. Nat responded by wrapping her arms around Maddy's waist and pulling her closer. It took her a moment to remember, they were not alone.

"Oh shit, Gino, I'm sorry man." Nat managed to say between kisses.

He laughed and turned up the radio. "I hear nothin,' I see nothin'. Home?"

"Yes please," Nat replied, Maddy's hands in her hair. He closed the partition separating them and pulled out onto the street.

Their kissing intensified, and Maddy took Nat's hand and brought it up the inside of her soft thigh, under her skirt, until Nat could feel Maddy's soaking panties. She gasped at the touch.

"You did that," Maddy purred. "You've been doing that to me every day since the day we met."

"Oh god," she whispered.

Maddy straddled Nat, her hand still in place. "Please," Maddy said, so softly, Nat wasn't sure if she meant for her to hear it.

"Wait…wait." She gently held Maddy a few inches away from her so she could look in her eyes. "I don't want to fuck you in the back of a car. I want to take my time with you. Savor this, remember?" She gave Maddy a cheeky grin and took a moment to brush one of Maddy's stray curls behind her ear. "Look at you. You are so damn beautiful. Let's wait until I can get you in my nice, soft bed."

Maddy looked at Nat like she couldn't believe what she was saying. Nat had a flash of panic that she had just screwed everything up. But then Maddy brought Nat's mouth to meet hers, and they began to slowly, deeply kiss. Just kiss. They explored each other's lips and tongues, all the way to Queens.

As Gino pulled up in front of Nat's apartment, she felt wonderfully dizzy and disoriented from kissing Maddy. Gino opened the car door and held out his hand to Maddy, who took a moment to straighten her skirt, while he averted his eyes. Nat slapped him on the shoulder and handed him three hundred dollars.

"Thank you, man. I owe you one." He laughed and gave Nat a knowing wink as he got back in the car and drove off.

Nat looked at Maddy, her red hair illuminated by the rising moon above. She grabbed Maddy's eager hand and pulled her inside the building. On the elevator ride up, they resumed their kissing, which had now escalated to a frenzy, knowing that Nat's bed wasn't far away. They stumbled down the hallway, and through the door to her apartment. Eddie made the mistake of getting underfoot and let out a meow of displeasure.

"Sorry, Ed," Nat panted.

Maddy pulled the leather jacket from her shoulders and ran her hands through the back of Nat's hair, gently tugging her head back to access her sensitive neck. The sensation of Maddy's hot tongue and teeth against her skin elicited a moan from Nat. She slid her hands down Maddy's sides and under her skirt. She cupped her ass and walked her backward until Maddy was up against the wall. She hooked her fingers into Maddy's panties.

"I just need a taste. Is that okay?" Nat whispered into Maddy's ear, as she slowly tugged her panties down.

"Oh, god. Natalia, what are you doing to me?" Maddy asked, breathlessly as Nat slowly descended the length of her body. After tossing her panties aside, she slowly rolled Maddy's skirt over her thighs, revealing what she hungered for. She pressed her lips to the top of Maddy's waiting sex, and her tongue gently trailed along across her hardening nub. Maddy sighed deeply and ran her hands through Nat's hair. Nat kissed and sucked for a moment and slid her way back up Maddy's body, kissing every part of skin left exposed until she held her face in her hands.

"I've never known anyone like you. I want to know every part of you," Nat said quietly.

"Then take me," Maddy replied, her eyes twinkling with desire.

Nat led her down the hallway into the bedroom. She made quick work of her dress, unzipping it and letting it fall to the floor. She undid her bra, exposing her full, pale breasts and taking one of the small, pink nipples into her mouth. It was as delicious as a ripe raspberry, and she lavished attention on both breasts. Maddy pulled Nat's T-shirt over her head, sidelining her busy mouth. Maddy yanked off Nat's belt with unexpected aplomb. She fiddled with her zipper, pushing her gently onto the bed. She peeled both Nat's jeans and underwear down her legs. At last, they were both naked. Maddy lowered herself on top of Nat, who spread her legs to accommodate Maddy's thigh as it slid between them.

"We fit perfectly together, don't you think?" Maddy asked while dipping her head to engulf one of Nat's hardened nipples. Maddy lifted her eyes to gaze at her new lover, Nat's breast firmly between her lips. Nat looked back, her mind overflowing with affection for this woman, her body on the verge of overload. She pulled Maddy's mouth back to her own.

As they found themselves in a deep kiss, so did their centers, causing them both to gasp with pleasure. They moved in rhythm against each other, careful not to lose contact, grasping each other tightly. It didn't take long before Nat began to feel the wave of climax wash over her. Hearing Maddy's screams of pleasure and feeling her body begin to tighten sent Nat over the edge. They came together and collapsed against each other. Maddy lay with her head against Nat's chest, while she gently ran her hand across Nat's breast. Nat played with Maddy's curls until they soon fell asleep in each other's arms.

CHAPTER TWENTY-TWO

Nat's eyelids fluttered at the sunlight streaming into the room. There was something in the air, something sweet and comforting that caused her mouth to water. She rolled over to see that Maddy wasn't next to her. Her stomach sank for a moment thinking she had left, not wanting to face Nat in the light of day after their night of passion.

Then she heard a clattering coming from the kitchen and was relieved to know she wasn't alone after all. She laid her head back and grinned, thinking of the night before. Maddy's sweet kisses, her hands in Nat's hair as she…

"Good morning, sleepyhead."

The vision of Maddy appeared, and her beauty in the sleepy haze of the room swept all other thoughts from Nat's mind. Maddy wore one of Nat's old well-worn and heather gray T-shirts, from a beloved band long broken up. A simple pair of black cotton panties gave Nat full view of her beautiful, pale legs. In her hands, a cup of coffee and a blueberry muffin. Not just any blueberry muffin, a freshly baked blueberry muffin.

Maddy set down the coffee, climbed on the bed and straddled Nat, muffin in hand.

"You looked so adorable. I didn't want to wake you." She stroked the exposed part of Nat's abdomen. "So, I thought I'd make you breakfast. Then I looked in your fridge… You know those things are supposed to contain food, right?"

Nat gave her a sly smile.

"Well, I took a little trip to the market down the street and they had these beautiful blueberries. Totally out of season, but I couldn't resist." Maddy tore off a chunk of the muffin.

"I can hardly resist, myself," Nat murmured hungrily as she ran her hands up Maddy's naked thighs. Maddy leaned in and placed the piece of muffin in Nat's waiting mouth. Her finger, stained purple from the berries at the tip, lingered on Nat's lips. Nat moaned her approval at the taste of the muffin. Sweet and still warm from the oven, blueberries bursting on her tongue.

"You really are some sort of wizard," she whispered. "Is it weird that I'm totally turned on by those goddamn muffins?"

Maddy threw back her head as she laughed and ran her hands up the length of Nat's torso. She had flour on her cheek, which Nat found so fantastically endearing.

Maddy brought her mouth close to her ear and whispered, "That was the point," before taking the lobe into her warm mouth. Nat gasped. Maddy's lips hovered over Nat's. She smelled like spearmint and spun sugar, Nat thought, wanting to breathe her in. Then reality set in.

"Oh my god, hold that thought. I haven't even brushed my teeth yet!" She gave Maddy a quick peck on the forehead before slipping out of bed and running to the bathroom.

Nat looked at herself in the mirror, and despite her disheveled hair and slightly smudged eye makeup, she beamed. She vigorously brushed her teeth, as two warm hands snaked around her stomach, underneath her tank top. She caught sight of Maddy smiling at her from behind her shoulder, and her hands wandered further up Nat's body. Maddy pressed her lips to the back of Nat's neck, just as her hands cupped Nat's breasts.

Desire welled inside Nat, and she spun around, grabbing Maddy by the waist. Maddy wiped away the water from Nat's mouth with her thumb. Nat crushed Maddy's lips with her own, as her tongue searched out Maddy's.

In one swift move, Nat peeled off Maddy's shirt and tossed it to the floor. She bent down, taking one of Maddy's hard sweet nipples in her mouth. Maddy sucked in a breath as Nat picked her up and sat her upon the vanity. Maddy straddled Nat and pulled their mouths together. Nat slid her hand under Maddy's panties, between her pink, wet folds.

"Yes, please, Natalia," Maddy managed to gasp between kisses. Nat obliged, running her fingers along Maddy's slick flesh, stopping to lavish attention on her throbbing clit. Maddy sunk her teeth into Nat's shoulder. Nat slowly moved from Maddy's clit to the edge of her opening. She slid in two fingers, and Maddy moaned. She pumped in and out, her fingers covered in Maddy's wetness. Maddy's back arched in the mirror and Nat couldn't remember seeing something quite so desirable before. She watched her fingers move in and out of her lover. A pang of white-hot desire shot through her body, aching for its own release. Maddy tightened around her fingers and Nat knew she was close. As the redhead climaxed, Maddy took Nat's face in her hands, never losing eye contact as she came in waves. Nat kept her fingers inside Maddy, even after the tremors subsided, and kissed her flushed cheeks and lips. Maddy collapsed against her, with delicious exhaustion.

After a moment, Nat broke the silence. "Those were some muffins."

Both women laughed and kissed each other until it was finally time to shower and do it all over again.

CHAPTER TWENTY-THREE

The next day in rehearsal, Nat couldn't stop smiling. She smiled when she broke a string. Smiled when Paul spilled bong water on the carpet. Smiled when her voice cracked on a high note from too little sleep and too much pleasure. She was even smiling when Paul and Jackie stopped playing and simply stared at her.

"Christ, Chambers. You're starting to freak us out with all this happiness," Paul announced. "Did Operation Seal the Deal work or are you on a lot of Xanax?"

Nat let out a delighted sigh and slid into the nearest chair. "Oh, the deal has been sealed. Many times. Many, many times."

Jackie dropped to a cross-legged sitting position in front of her. "I'm absolutely chuffed, Nat! Aren't you chuffed, Paul?"

"I have no idea what that means, Jackie, but I am certainly happy for our dear ol' Chambers. Tell us everything," he said.

Nat shook her head but continued to smile. "I'm a lady. I would never besmirch my reputation or Maddy's by divulging such intimate details." She grabbed a pillow and screamed into it, "But I really, really want to!"

"Well, all that matters is that you're happy and you seem… refreshed." Jackie said.

"Refreshed?" Paul asked. "She looks like she was fucked by an angel. And yes, that is an actual porn. It's less awkward than you would imagine."

"Paul, do you even just, not?" Jackie asked.

He shrugged.

Nat kept smiling. "For real, though, it was amazing and as much as I want to shout from the mountains how she made me feel, I also really respect her so I'm going to have to keep it zipped."

Paul rolled his eyes, but Jackie nodded. "We totally understand, don't we, Paul?" Jackie said.

He softened. "Of course, we do. Well, Jackie, it looks like our Natalia has found herself a muse."

To Nat, the days fell into a glorious routine. She spent a lot of her time in the studio, but when Maddy's busy schedule allowed, she was quick to spend quality time with her. They had been seeing each other for nearly three months and she couldn't get enough of the beautiful and sweet chef. Maddy had tough hours, which actually pushed Nat to work harder herself. With the European tour just around the corner, she needed it too. She was starting to find her place in the music again, and while she wasn't exactly churning out the hits, she felt close to a breakthrough.

While Nat was in the studio alone, plunking out notes on the piano, her phone buzzed with a message from Maddy.

Closing up soon. Want to meet me at the restaurant?

Her heart still fluttered every time she got a message from Maddy, and she quickly locked up the studio and headed to the city to meet. When she arrived, she could see the Touché crew tidying up and Maddy saying her goodbyes to her staff. She emerged from the restaurant in a pair of linen shorts that showed off her lovely legs and a black tank top. The weather was getting hotter and she was happy to see as much of Maddy's skin as possible. When Maddy saw her outside, she wrapped Nat in a tight embrace.

"Mmm, hi baby," Maddy said.

Nat loved it when Maddy called her baby. "Hi yourself. Want to go do something or do you want to head to my place," Nat asked, untangling herself from the blissful kiss.

"It's late," Maddy commented. "Why don't we go to my place?"

In the time that they'd been dating, Nat had never been inside Maddy's place. "Wow, this is like, a big deal. Seeing your place."

Maddy poked her in the ribs. "Hey, stop it. I'm hardly ever there and it's super small. Your place is much better. It's just close, and I don't know, I thought it was long overdue."

Nat offered her hand. "To Casa Maddy."

They strolled the streets of the Lower East Side in no real hurry. When they reached Maddy's, it was after midnight and the building was shrouded in dim light. She lived in a fourth-floor walk-up, which would partly explain her killer legs. When they reached the door, Maddy stopped her.

"Okay, it's really small."

"So you mentioned," Nat laughed.

Maddy smiled and gave the sticky door a push with her hip as she turned the key. The apartment was cozy. It was a studio with tall white walls and huge windows that looked out to the city. She could see why Maddy picked the place. In addition to its proximity to Touché, it had charm. It was exceptionally clean and cutely but sparsely decorated. A tiny kitchen shared space with the living room area, a queen-size bed tucked into the corner by a window.

"I'm going to hop in the shower really quick, okay?" Maddy kissed her on the cheek. "There's a kettle in the cupboard. Make us some tea?"

Maddy headed into the bathroom. She offered a knowing smile and left the door open so Nat could catch a glimpse of her naked form slipping into the shower.

She found the kettle and the herbal tea. While the water boiled, she toured the apartment, looking at the few things Maddy obviously cherished. A tiny bookshelf with some dog-eared novels. A record player. Portraits of Paris. On a shelf near the bed was a lovely framed picture of a red-haired woman holding a toddler and smiling. The same smile as Maddy. Maddy's mom. Nat ran her finger lightly over the glass, removing any accumulating dust.

"She was a knockout, wasn't she?" Maddy gently toweled her hair, wearing just underwear and a loose T-shirt. "When I left, I wasn't able to take much. It's the only picture I have of the two of us."

"Well, I know where you get it from now," Nat said. "We haven't really talked much about your mom. How does talking about her make you feel?"

Maddy tossed the towel on a nearby chair. "Oh, I love talking about her. You don't have to worry about upsetting me."

The kettle whistled and Nat returned to the kitchen to fill their mugs. "Peppermint or lemon?"

"Peppermint, please."

They settled into Maddy's love seat with their tea, and Maddy sighed in relief.

"So, tell me about her. What was she like?" Nat asked before burning the tip of her tongue on the piping hot tea.

"Well, she was beautiful. That you can see. I always thought she was some kind of princess. She just lit up the room. She was soft-spoken. And kind, very kind. She was a kindergarten teacher before she had me so she had a natural temperament for kindness." Maddy blew on her tea but didn't yet drink. "I was so young when she died that all I have of her are slivers of memories. A flash here and there. I know she loved me and I know I felt safe with her. She loved my dad too, for all his stubbornness. They were high school sweethearts." Maddy seemed to pull thoughts of her mother from the background of her mind.

"Can I ask... What happened?"

Maddy sighed. "Aneurysm. A freak thing. One day she was fine and the next day my dad found her unconscious in the flower garden."

Her heart sank, trying to put herself in Maddy's shoes. "Maddy, I'm so sorry."

Maddy reached out and caressed her face. "Baby, you have nothing to be sorry for. It happened, and it was terrible, but she loved me and that's what I keep in my heart."

"You are something else, Madeline LaDuke," Nat said, leaning back to take Maddy all in—her wet curls brushing her shoulders, her bright eyes, and a heart that knew pain but chose to focus on love.

"Okay," Maddy said, smiling at Nat's obvious affection. "What were you like as a kid?"

Nat laughed. "Oh, man. Well, I was…artistic. That's a good word for it. Also intense. Very intense for a young person."

Maddy stifled a giggle. "I can totally see that."

"You can, can you?" She picked up one of Maddy's feet, placed it on her lap, and rubbed away. "Yeah, imagine me, basically being this, bangs and all, but like, ten."

"You poor, poor, thing," Maddy cooed. "Mmm, that feels amazing, don't stop. When did you lose your virginity?"

"Nice segue," Nat teased. "Really, you want to go there?"

"Yup."

"Fine. Okay, I was eighteen. It was my freshman year of college. She was my TA for music theory."

Maddy sat up. "Whoa! Now that's saucy. You basically lost your virginity to your teacher?"

"No, she was my TA. A grad student. She was twenty-two and it wasn't that big of a deal."

"Did you get an A?"

"I got a B. But it had nothing to do with it," she said, feeling her face turn red with embarrassment.

Maddy wiggled her eyebrows. "Hot for teacher. You little minx."

She sighed, knowing Maddy was getting a kick out of her reaction. "Fine. What about you?"

Maddy chewed on her bottom lip for a moment. "I was… twenty? She was a German tourist who swept me off my feet for about seventy-two hours. We did it in her hotel room the night before she left to go back home."

"Wow, that's kind of romantic. And sad."

"Oh, it wasn't sad to me. I was in no place emotionally to get involved with someone. I hadn't even looked at another girl since I'd left home. It was…a blessing. It was sweet, and it felt good and there were no expectations. It did at least confirm to me that I liked girls and that would always be a part of me."

"What was her name?"

Maddy looked at her thoughtfully before answering. "Frederica. Freddie."

She raised her cup of tea. "To Freddie, who gave you a wonderful gift."

Maddy leaned over and kissed her. "You never cease to amaze me, Natalia. You are the only person I know who would propose a toast to the woman who took my virginity."

She shrugged. "We all have a history. It makes us who we are. Okay, back to you, Pastry Princess. What's your absolute favorite thing to make?"

She looked exasperated. "That's like asking me to pick my favorite kid."

"Do you have children?"

"Oh yeah, you didn't notice them in the front closet?" She smiled. "Well, I love those cookies I made for you that first night."

"Best cookies I've ever had. In my life. I swear to Betty Crocker," Nat said, with her hand over her heart.

"Thank you, I love them too. But if I had to choose it would be *pain au chocolat*."

"Why?"

"Because they take a lot of work. You have to be careful. All the elements have to be right. If the butter melts too soon, you won't get those beautiful layers. You'll end up with a bready mess. It takes patience and practice. Then you have this piece of bittersweet chocolate that comes in and shakes things up. Elevates it. I love that bitter, sweet and buttery element."

"God, now I'm starving. And sort of turned on."

"Well, then I'm doing something right. Now, tell me, why did you leave Nashville?"

"Good question. I just didn't feel like I belonged there. I mean, don't get me wrong. Nashville is great. It's a fun place and the talent there is amazing. You can't even go to an open mic without hearing the next big thing. But I often felt like something wasn't clicking. I was writing a lot for other people, as you know, and it was satisfying to a point. Then one day, I was at the Bluebird watching someone sing a song I wrote, and I started crying. It was beautiful, but it wasn't mine anymore. I didn't want to keep handing my songs—my dreams—away to someone else. So I came to NYC and it's hard and it's dirty and the people aren't always nice, but it's where I need to be. New York reminds me every day of what's at stake, and I need that in my life. And Maddy, I have to tell you something and I hope it doesn't change the way you feel about me."

Maddy's brow furrowed. "What is it?"

She swallowed hard. "I hate...herbal tea."

Maddy threw her head back laughing. "You shit! Why didn't you say something?"

"I didn't want to lose my lesbian street cred. They love tea. I feel like such a failure."

"Oh baby, don't worry about that because you are super gay," Maddy said as she bopped her on the nose.

"Thank god. I would hate to think that all those lessons my parents paid for had gone to waste."

"No more herbal tea. I promise."

"You're a lifesaver."

She switched out her tea for a seltzer and the two talked until three a.m. before Maddy's eyes were heavy and it was time to go to sleep.

"Stay the night," Maddy said before she leaned in and kissed Nat again.

"Okay."

Nat stripped down to her underwear and crawled under the comforter with Maddy.

"Nat?"

"Mmm?"

"Like, no tea at all or just herbal tea?" Maddy asked, her eyes closed but a smile on her face.

"Go to sleep, beautiful," Nat said as she squeezed Maddy tight.

CHAPTER TWENTY-FOUR

"I don't know. I think we have a tight set already and I'm not sure I would change anything about it," Nat said as she popped a spicy tuna roll into her mouth.

Nat, Jackie, and Paul sat at a sushi spot close to the studio, finalizing their set before they headed to Europe. They would play Philadelphia the next day and then head straight to London after the show.

Paul tossed back his sake. "Yeah, I agree. It's a good set. I don't think the audiences there are quite as familiar with our stuff as the ones here, so let's stick to the songs we know are hits with any audience."

"Works for me," Jackie added as she picked up a piece of sashimi and dunked it in soy sauce.

"Jackie, are your parents going to come to our London show?" Nat asked.

Jackie rolled her eyes. "I don't know. They want to see me, but they're still not keen on this rock business."

"Bring them to me. I'll charm their pants off," Paul offered.

"Paul darling, I don't want to scare them any more than they are already. This is…" She waved her hand in a circle in Paul's direction "…a lot."

Nat laughed. She was excited about introducing a new audience to the band, but she had a little lump in her throat when she thought of not seeing Maddy for nearly a month, but that was the life of a musician. Thankfully, Maddy understood and respected that.

Paul tapped on the table. "Nat, you know Oliver and the label will want a full album of new material by the time we get back." She twisted her mouth into a grimace. "I get it. We all go through it. If I could write the stuff I would, but I don't have your skills. We've got to pull together and get this new album ready or we're screwed. I know you need a muse or whatever, so how come now that you have Maddy, you're still not writing? I don't want to be *that* guy, but you wrote like crazy when you were with Melissa."

Paul's words stung like an angry swarm of bees. What he said had weighed on Nat for a while now. She thought she had found her muse in Maddy, but right now the songs were still just floating around her head unfinished. What was she doing wrong? She was so happy but she wasn't creating anything. She needed to buckle down and figure this out.

She nodded at Paul, even as it hurt to look him in the eye. "Yeah, I know. I really do. I don't want to let any of you down. We'll have an album. I promise."

CHAPTER TWENTY-FIVE

Nat hovered over a naked Maddy, planting kisses on her neck. Maddy shivered with delight as she zeroed in on the sensitive spot right beneath her jaw.

"Mmm, what am I going to do without you for three weeks?" Maddy purred.

Nat made her way lower and peppered Maddy's breasts and abdomen with feather-soft kisses.

Maddy continued. "How am I going to make it a day without seeing your gorgeous face and your crazy hair?" Maddy playfully fluffed Nat's bangs.

She flicked her smiling eyes to Maddy, as she ventured even lower.

"And that thing you do with your ton...oh." Her voice trailed off as Nat demonstrated her point. Nat made love to Maddy for the next half hour, knowing she was pushing her luck with her travel schedule, but not giving a damn. She lavished attention on her body, running her tongue slowly from Maddy's clit to her opening, then plunging inside her, causing Maddy to thrash and moan. She sucked and licked and took her sweet time until Maddy came, glistening with perspiration. She kissed away the tiny beads of sweat between her breasts. Salty and sweet, and perfectly Maddy.

When Maddy couldn't take anymore, Nat settled beside her, covering her gently with a sheet. Then she took Maddy's face in her hands and kissed her softly. "I will call as often as I can, and I'll email and text you all the time. You will be completely sick of me by the time I get back."

Maddy pushed her shoulder playfully. "I couldn't get sick of you, Natalia. You walked right in and set up shop in my heart." Maddy paused, her eyes softening. "I like you. Like, really like you."

Nat stared back at the beautiful woman in her bed, exposed inside and out. She was flooded with emotion. Was she hoping for an "I love you" or relieved that Maddy hadn't gone there yet? She could feel her pulse pounding in her ears, her neck, her toes. After so many wrong calls and disappointments, she had given up hope that something magical was possible. But now, this amazing creature beside her was giving herself completely to Nat. This was turning into something that looked and felt a lot like love. She took a deep breath. Nat took Maddy's hand and kissed each knuckle. She gazed back into Maddy's hazel eyes. She felt so much affection pulsing through her body. Nat knew she loved Maddy. "I really, really like you too, Madeline."

CHAPTER TWENTY-SIX

Nat was invigorated from the show. For all her bitching and moaning about going back on tour, the stage was where she came to life. Now she also had something to come home to—Maddy. She slid, exhausted but content, into her dressing room chair. Jackie and Paul would be drinking beer and doing shots with the crew in the green room and she needed a few minutes to breathe. They would be taking the early flight to Heathrow in the morning, and she was debating just pushing through the night so she could sleep on the flight. She picked up her phone and smiled to see a voice mail from Maddy waiting for her. Before she had a chance to press play, there was a knock at the door. She called over her shoulder, "Come on in, it's open."

"Great show, Natalia. Nice to see you haven't lost your touch."

Her stomach dropped when she heard the unmistakable voice. She turned in her chair to face Melissa Hartford, who stood in the doorway, arms crossed. She wore tan cowboy boots and a dress covered with a daisy print, her dark hair much shorter than Nat remembered.

"Going for the hipster Laura Ingalls Wilder look these days, Mel?"

Melissa chortled and licked her bottom lip. "You always did make me laugh, Nat."

She shifted in her seat, irritation rising within her. "So, what do I owe this…this?"

"Well, I saw the show. I like your new lineup." Melissa's words were lined with daggers.

"Yeah, I kind of needed a change. Jackie's fantastic. I'm very lucky."

"Are you fucking her?" Melissa asked, without any emotion on her face.

Nat was taken aback. "Well, not that it's any of your goddamn business, but no. She's straight anyway."

"Hmm, give it time. That's always been my experience."

She stood, uncomfortable with the direction of the conversation, and leaned against the dressing table. "Why are you here?"

"I'm sorry. We got off on the wrong foot. There's always been something about you that sets me to extremes. You look good, Nat. Are you well?"

"I'm good. You cut your hair."

Her hair was now cut close on the side, curls cascading over her forehead. She brushed a few strands aside and looked back at Nat, her eyes flashing. She had always loved the blue-gray shade of her eyes, but now she just thought they looked cold, like a frozen lake or the ocean right before you drown.

"You know," Melissa said as she picked at some flaking paint on the door frame, "There was something about you tonight. You seemed, I don't know, especially energized."

"You'd be surprised what nearly a year without seeing your girlfriend go down on your best friend will do to a person's attitude." Nat said, her voice flat.

Melissa pursed her lips and nodded. "I deserve that. I do. You know Lara didn't mean anything to me. It was just a moment."

"And somehow, that makes it ten times worse," she responded, adding a fresh coat of lip balm.

"Okay, can we please start this conversation over?" Melissa asked, her eyes less cold now.

Nat shrugged. "Fine."

"Nat...Natalia... I know that Oliver spoke to you about a possible joint tour. I want you to give it another thought."

She stiffened and crossed her arms. "There's nothing to think about."

"Listen, my last studio album didn't perform as well as I'd hoped."

"Well, maybe that's because you were busy performing other things." She hoped that stung, and from the look on Melissa's face, it did. "I'm sorry, I truly am. You are a talented musician, Melissa. I'm sure things will turn around for you."

"Despite everything, you can't pretend that we don't have something special on stage, Nat."

"Had something," she corrected.

Melissa sighed, her hands dropping to her sides. "I just think this could really be mutually beneficial, boost both our sales and—"

"I don't care about the money."

"Damn it, Nat! It's not just about the money!" Melissa pounded on the door frame.

Nat was surprised by her outburst. Melissa took a few steps toward her. "I fucked up, okay? I fucked it all up. I'm a life ruiner. I broke your heart and I broke my own. Just please, please don't shut me out right now."

For a moment, Nat felt a pang of sympathy for Melissa. She reached out a hand and touched Melissa on the arm to comfort her. "We can't change the past. No need to beat yourself up about it. It's over now," she said softly, patting her arm.

Melissa looked up at her. "It doesn't have to be."

With that, Melissa kissed her on the lips. Nat was shocked and leaned back until her head hit the mirror behind her, hoping it would break the kiss, but it didn't. Suddenly, her head filled with memories of Melissa. The taste of juniper on her lips from the gin and tonics she so loved. How the perfect blend of their voices would send a shiver down her spine whenever they sang together that summer.

Then as quickly as it came, the feeling dissolved into little pebbles of memories, raining down and skipping in all directions until her head was clear again. She gently pushed Melissa back. When she looked over Melissa's shoulder, she saw a figure in the doorway. Maddy stood there, looking as if she'd been shot through the heart. She turned on her heels and walked out of sight.

"Shit!" Nat swore and chased after her, down the dark hallway that smelled of stale beer and mildew. She caught Maddy's elbow before she reached the stairs but Maddy wrenched out of Nat's grasp. Her eyes were wet with tears.

"Maddy, that was not what it looked like. I swear to god!"

"I am so stupid. So, fucking stupid!" she spat between sobs.

"No! You're amazing! It was just a misunderstanding. Please let me explain…"

"I don't know what I was thinking, falling in love with a musician. I always knew there was a possibility that you'd cheat on me while you were bored and lonely on tour. I just didn't think it would happen on the first goddamn night!"

"Whoa, Maddy sweetie, you have it all wrong."

"That was Melissa Hartford, wasn't it?"

Nat paused. "Yes."

She laughed angrily. "Perfect. How am I supposed to compete with that anyway? She gets you, doesn't she? Me? I'm just a boring girl from Montana that bakes you fucking muffins." She turned and walked up the stairs. Nat was beside herself, not knowing what else to say.

"But I love your muffins! I love you! Please, don't leave!" Nat shouted after her but it was too late. She slipped through the stage door and disappeared into the crowd. Nat held her head in her hands, kicking the wall with her heel. She had no idea how everything had gotten so sideways. She didn't want Melissa. All she wanted was Maddy, and now she was gone.

She walked back to the dressing room to find Melissa still waiting for her, sitting in her chair. Now this time, Nat stood in the doorway.

"Wow, well that was awkward," Melissa said, pushing a strand of hair behind her ear.

"You know, you were right, Melissa," Nat said quietly, her eyes downward.

Melissa smiled at Nat's admission. "Yeah?"

"Yeah," she replied, lifting her eyes to meet Melissa's. "You are a life ruiner. Now kindly get the hell out of my dressing room." She gestured to the door. Taken aback, Melissa got up slowly and walked past Nat without another word. Nat closed the door behind her and sat down. Her voicemail from Maddy was right there on her phone's home screen. She pushed play.

"Hi baby, so I couldn't help myself! Paul got me into the show, so I drove to Philly! I wanted one more kiss before you fly across the ocean. I know you're going to be amazing. I'll be out there, cheering you on. Break a leg. Paul will bring me backstage after the show. I can't wait to see you… I love you. I love you like crazy. Okay, bye!"

Nat saved the message and pushed the phone away.

"Fuck."

CHAPTER TWENTY-SEVEN

They were halfway through their flight to London and the plane was quiet except for an occasional cough or snore. Nat hadn't slept a wink, despite the Klonopin and Jack and Coke she hoped would push away the awful memory of Maddy's tear-stained face. Across the aisle, Jackie slept peacefully with her eye mask and neck pillow perfectly placed. Next to her, Paul's face was bathed in the soft glow of his computer screen. He was engrossed in whatever show he was binge-watching.

She had tried calling and texting Maddy all the way to the airport, but there was no response. Paul and Jackie, who it seemed never stopped talking, were uncharacteristically quiet as the trio sat at the gate. Paul had apologized for not telling Nat that Maddy was going to be there, but he couldn't have anticipated how the night would play out. Nat knew it was no one's fault but her own. And Melissa's. But she should have told Melissa to leave right away. She could have stepped away when Melissa leaned closer. Coulda woulda shoulda. Now Maddy, the girl that made her heart sing harmony, had run away from her. The thought of causing Maddy pain made her wince in her seat. Paul must have seen her reaction because he slipped off his headphones and reached over and put his warm hand on her forearm.

"It's going to be okay. She'll come around. That girl loves you like crazy."

The kindness of his words broke the dam of emotion welling inside her since she watched Maddy leave. Fat, hot tears fell out of her eyes and onto the blank notebook paper that sat untouched in front of her on the fold-out tray.

"But... What if she doesn't. What if she hates me now? Pauley, what if I lost her?" She choked back a new flood of tears, trying to keep her voice down and not disturb the slumbering passengers.

"Give her a little space," he whispered.

"I'm flying to fucking Jolly Old England right now! I think that's enough space," she whispered back, frustration straining in her words.

He pursed his lips. "I don't mean literal space. Metaphorical space, Chambers."

She narrowed her teary eyes at him.

"Sorry, I shouldn't kick a girl when she's down. She's hurt. She feels foolish. Give her some time to think about things. Calling her drunk and sad from Düsseldorf or some shit like that..."

"Düsseldorf?"

"I did not look at the itinerary. I like to live spontaneously. Whatever. You are missing my point."

"And that would be?"

He pointed to the notebook in front of her. "That you need to pour everything you want to say to Maddy on that piece of paper like the goddamn lesbian singer/songwriter you are. Use it, Nat. The pain you're feeling will be your symphony. Put it there. Not into endless and embarrassing text messages and voice mails. Give Maddy the space to remember why she was so crazy about you in the first place."

With that, he poked her tray for emphasis, slipped his headphones back on, and turned his attention back to the screen. She pulled out the pen that was stuck in the notepad's spiral binding, took a deep breath, wiped her eyes, and started to write.

CHAPTER TWENTY-EIGHT

It was in Berlin, not Düsseldorf, where the band ended the tour three weeks later, and where Nat pulled up a seat at a dark bar that smelled of tobacco and weed but somehow suited her mood. She'd had no response from Maddy, but as Paul had advised, she'd given her space, as much as it just tightened the knot in her gut.

Their shows in London, Amsterdam and Barcelona had gone off all right. They were in no way her best performances, with her throat often dry from crying and too much whiskey, but the audiences had been forgiving, and their energy helped get her through. If anything good came out of her separation from Maddy, it was that she was writing. A lot. She'd already filled a notebook with new lyrics and chords and slipped into this Berlin bar to write some more and have a beer. Paul and Jackie had expressed concern about her boozing that week, so she was trying to take it easy. One thing she knew: she wouldn't find forgiveness at the bottom of a whiskey glass. She was scribbling away when she felt someone standing in front of her.

"*Möchtest du was trinken?*" asked the bartender, who had a short blond bob and blood red lipstick pulled across a sexy smile. She looked up and under different circumstances, she'd do some flirting, but all she could think about was Maddy.

"*Ein bier, bitte.* Whatever you recommend." The bartender nodded and pulled on the tap. She slid the mug over to Nat, who took it in her eager hands. She took a long slug of the bitter, skunky ale and continued her writing. Soon she felt the stool next to her swivel, and the familiar form of Paul sat down beside her. He pointed to her beer and motioned to the bartender that he'd like one of the same. They sat in silence for a bit, sipping their beers, enjoying the anonymity of the quiet bar, which was interrupted when his cell phone buzzed, and his face lit up at the text. She realized in that moment that she was so absorbed in her own drama, she hadn't really checked in with her bandmates.

"That's some smile," Nat observed.

"Yeah, well…" He blushed, something she could never recall him doing before when it came to a guy.

"Whoa. Wait. Are you into someone?"

He sighed. "I don't know. Maybe. Yes."

"When did this happen?"

"That night we played with Redfern. I met this guy named Ryder, and well, he's really great. He's smart and funny, and I don't know what to do because I'm an asshole and he's kind of perfect."

She couldn't help but laugh. "But you are a lovable asshole! So, this Ryder, he was the cute guy I saw you with that night?"

He nodded. "Yeah, he's so fucking dreamy."

She nodded. "From what I remember, dreamboat city."

He took a sip of his beer. "He transitioned a few years ago and has been working at a nonprofit ever since." He paused, waiting for Nat to respond.

"Yeah?"

"I mean, he's super out and everything. He would be okay with me telling you. He's a big activist for LGBTQ rights."

"He sounds pretty spectacular."

He got a far-off look in his eye. "Yeah, he is. He's just so kind and sexy. When we're lying in bed afterward, I don't want to leave. I want to cuddle up in his arms, trace his tattoos with my fingers, and never let him go."

She felt a lump form in her throat. He was in love and he didn't even realize it yet.

"Well," she said, raising her glass. "I can't wait to officially meet Ryder when we get back and give him a big squeeze." This made Paul smile. "I'm sorry."

He cocked his head. "For what, Chambers?"

"For being a shitty friend these last couple weeks. I'm sorry I was so caught up in my own heartache that I didn't notice you were happy. I'm sorry you didn't feel you could share your happiness with me."

He reached over and put his arm around her shoulders. "You are my family, Nat. You're the only person I've ever really let my guard down with. You were going through something pretty fucking terrible, and it's okay. That's what I'm here for. I'm your bear. Your big gay, Korean bear."

With this, she burst out laughing, for the first time in weeks. It felt so damn good.

CHAPTER TWENTY-NINE

It was eight thirty a.m. Paris time when Nat stood above her slumbering bandmates and cleared her throat. Loudly. The band had played a sold-out show in the Marias neighborhood the night before, and she was actually starting to feel a little spark of herself again. They were set to depart back home that night, but before they left, she needed to do something and she wanted Jackie and Paul to join her.

When the throat clearing didn't work, she gently nudged the pair who had fallen asleep together in Paul's bed, sweetly snoring and wearing their clothes from the night before. Jackie stirred, blinking her chocolate brown eyes at Nat with their long, enviable lashes.

"Good god, Nat, what bloody time is it?" Jackie asked, her voice groggy with sleep.

"It's eight thirty."

"That's obscene," Jackie said with a sneer.

"I know, but I need your and Sleeping Beauty's help on something today. Can you wake him?"

Jackie sighed and rolled over to face Paul, who had a small puddle of drool forming on his pillow. "Paul. Pauley." Jackie gently pushed his shoulder. "Paul darling, they have croissants and mar-i-jua-na downstairs, for free."

He snorted and looked around the room. "What? Where? Hi, Nat."

"*Bon matin*, Paul."

He picked up his phone to look at the time. "I swear to Liza, someone better be dead if you are trying to wake us up this early, Chambers."

She sat on the bed as Jackie and Paul lazily wiped sleep from their eyes. "So, I need your help today. I need to find a patisserie in the 10th arrondissement."

"Um, there's a bakery, like, right downstairs," Paul said.

Jackie looked at her thoughtfully. "You want to find Maddy's patisserie, don't you?"

She nodded.

"Maddy's patisserie?" Paul asked.

Jackie huffed and looked at him. "Don't you pay attention, you knob? It's where Maddy learned how to bake! She lived with this older couple and he taught her before she went to culinary school."

"How do you even know that?" he asked.

"Because I'm a woman and I'm thoughtful," she said with a wink. "I don't recall the name, though."

"That's the problem. She never told me the name. All I know is it's in the 10th arrondissement and it has a living quarters above it."

He picked up his vape and took a long drag. "Well, shit, there's got to be dozens of patis...patisis..."

"Patisseries," Nat and Jackie said in unison.

"Right, there have to be dozens."

"Well, I've narrowed it down to eight," Nat said. "If we get moving, we can hit them all."

"What is the endgame here, Nat?" Paul asked.

"Honestly, I don't really have one. I just want to see the place that helped make Maddy who she is. Even if I never see her again, I want to understand her."

Jackie swooned. "Goddamn, that's romantic."

Paul nodded in agreement. "Let me find my pants."

After walking the streets of Paris for a few hours, Nat, Jackie and Paul stood in front of a quaint storefront with a second story. The hand painted sign said Le Patisserie de Carm, and as soon as Nat stood in front of it, she knew this was the right place. The upstairs featured a window with a small balcony. She could picture Maddy sitting at the window and dreaming away.

"This is it," Nat said.

"How do you know?" Paul asked.

"I just do."

They pushed through the heavy door into the shop, its small bell chiming, and they were immediately hit with the smell of fresh baked baguettes and buttery croissants. It was the smell that had captured Maddy's senses when she'd first moved here. Nat breathed it in as much as she could.

"*Bonjour*," a voice called. A man who appeared to be in his sixties emerged from the backroom. "*Puis je t'aider?*"

"Bonjour," Nat said. "*Excusez moi, parlez-vous anglais?*"

The man nodded. "*Oui.* How can I help you?"

Her heart was in her throat. "Um, did you have an apprentice named Maddy LaDuke?"

A broad smile broke out on his face. "*Oui*, Madeline!"

Paul let out a sigh of relief while Jackie was transfixed by the pastry case.

"That's wonderful. We know Madeline. We're…friends of hers in New York."

"Ah, *ma petite* Madeline," he said. "You know, I taught her everything I know. But she is something special, no? Didn't take her long until she was surpassing me. A lesser man would be jealous, but no, not me. I am proud." She could tell by the way he beamed that he was indeed.

"I'm Nat, and this is Paul and Jackie."

"*Je suis* Philipe Bouchard. My wife Carm is out right now, but she would have loved to meet friends of Madeline's. Come, see," Phillipe said as he brought them over to a picture hanging on their wall. There was a fresh-faced Maddy, a white chef's cap sitting atop her shorter, cropped hair. She was being hugged by Phillipe and Carm, and her face was full of joy.

Tears welled in Nat's eyes as Phillipe continued. "We speak to Madeline every Christmas day. She is always being by herself, never with family. She has been through a lot of pain, no?"

Nat nodded and a tear dropped onto her shirt. "Yeah, she has."

Phillipe sniffed and tapped the wall next to the picture. "Yet, she finds a way. When you see her, will you please tell her the Bouchards send much love."

"Of course." She took his hand. It had the same small nicks and burns that Maddy's did. Baker's hands.

"Would you like anything? It is, as you say in America, on the house?"

Paul and Jackie's eyes widened. Phillipe laughed and filled a brown paper bag with breads and sweets.

"Thank you, Phillipe," Nat said. "You are too kind."

"I'm just glad to know that Madeline has people who care for her," he replied. "And you," he gestured to Nat. "I can see that you care for her very much indeed."

She let out a small, sad laugh. "I do, but I think I may have unintentionally hurt her very badly."

As Paul and Jackie devoured their spoils between "mmms" and "*mercis*" Phillipe pulled Nat aside. "Madeline learned to survive by putting up the barricades when she is wounded. I do not think she believes she deserves happiness, and when she is disappointed, she retreats. It is human nature to protect oneself, no?"

"You're right."

"If you care for Madeline, and want what's best for her, your heart will tell you what to do."

She nodded. "How'd you get so good at this advice thing?"

"I have been married for thirty years to a wonderful woman, and she has taught me the language of the heart. I have made many mistakes but we have always found our way back."

Jackie tapped Nat on the shoulder. "Mate, I'm sorry but we have to get headed to the airport." She motioned to the *pain au chocolat* in her hand. "And you, Phillipe, are a brilliant baker."

He nodded and took Nat's hands in his again. "Safe travels to all of you. And thank you for stopping by my humble little shop."

As the group headed out, Phillipe called out to Nat. "*Nat, 'Il n'y a qu'un bonheur dans la vie, c'est d'aimer et d'être aimé.'*

"What does that mean?" she asked.

"There is only one happiness in life: to love and to be loved. *Au revoir.*"

"*Au revoir.*"

She walked out into the sunny Paris day, the scent of bread still in her nose. She was hopeful and resigned at the same time. If she and Maddy were meant to be, love would find a way.

"Natalia," Paul called out, "Take this baguette and stand in front of the sign."

She stood next to the wooden sign on its rusty hinges. A well-loved place that showed love to Maddy, too. She took a deep breath and posed for the picture.

"Say *frommage*," Paul yelled.

"Absolutely not," she said as she smiled in spite of herself.

CHAPTER THIRTY

The Heathrow airport terminal buzzed with activity as passengers rushed to catch planes to destinations around the world. The bandmates sat in a row near their gate waiting for their transfer as muffled announcements called out overhead.

"Anyone want some chocolate? I think I need some," Jackie announced as she stood and stretched. Wearing comfy yoga pants and a Nat Chambers Band hoodie, she looked like she could crawl into any space and fall right asleep. Nat suddenly imagined Jackie snoozing in the overhead bin.

"Nah, I'm good," Nat said. "Oh, but I could mess up some Jelly Babies."

Jackie put her hands on her hips. "Come on, Nat. You find yourself in London and you choose not to partake in our far superior chocolate? You choose bloody Jelly Babies?"

"What can I say? I love a good gummy."

Paul grumbled. "Do they have any candy with crunchy Xanax bits in it?"

"I will check," Jackie said with a wink. "I might have to venture to duty free."

"Oh, wait, before you go," Nat said, "I was going to show you when we got home but I think now's the right time." Nat rustled around in her bag and pulled out her black notebook. She handed it to Jackie.

"Okay, it's your notebook," Jackie said.

Paul rose up in his seat and a big smile spread across his face. "No, Jackie my love. That's our new album."

She let out a huge sigh of relief. "There are fifteen new songs. Well, songlings. They aren't really songs until we collaborate on them but here they are. The songlings are ready to take flight."

Jackie let out a little squeal then ran off without a word.

"I knew you could do it, Chambers," Paul said, reaching over his hand to high-five her.

"Oh, Paul, I put my guts on the page. It's different than what we've done in the past. It's... I don't want to say deep, because that is beyond pretentious, but I pulled it out note by note from way down inside me."

He wrapped his arm around her and squeezed her tightly. "My baby's all grown up."

"Shut up. There's one I really want to show you." She flipped the page to a certain song and handed it to him. He was quiet for a moment while he took it in.

"Wow, this is, well, this is it, Nat. This is fucking it."

Jackie bounded back with three mini champagne bottles in her hands. "Here! This calls for a celebration."

They each carefully undid the foil wrapping and popped their tiny corks, laughing at the display.

Paul raised his bottle. "To friends and bandmates, to ecstasy and pain, to learning and living, and making new music."

The trio clinked their bottles and drank the cheap champagne like it was from the spring of eternal life.

CHAPTER THIRTY-ONE

Nat was dealing with a serious case of jet lag after returning home from tour. Her eyes ached, and Eddie demanded some serious head butts. She was about to order delivery from her favorite Thai place when her phone buzzed with a message from Paul.

Chambers, get your ass to Icon asap. You'll never believe who just walked in with some of her work friends.

Nat's hand trembled as she held the phone. Maddy was at Icon, the Brooklyn bar and live music venue where Nat had cut her teeth all those years ago. She stood frozen in her living room. Should she go and try to talk to Maddy? No. It had been nearly a month with no communication and Nat wanted to respect her space. But, what if seeing each other would make a difference? Her thumb hovered over Paul's text. Before she could respond, she saw the familiar little texting dots on his side of the conversation.

Stop overthinking, Natalia. This is your chance. And bring your guitar.

Paul was suggesting a grand gesture that could completely blow up in her face, but Maddy was worth the possible humiliation. She grabbed her jacket and her Martin guitar, kissed Eddie on the head, and headed out the door.

When she got to Icon, the place was already a flurry of people drinking, laughing, and talking. She came in through the side entrance as Paul suggested via text on her taxi ride over, since Maddy and her crew from the restaurant were in the front of the bar. She was greeted by Hinata, the proprietress of Icon and an old friend. They hugged and exchanged pleasantries. Paul, now joined by Jackie, had already filled her in on the plan.

"Okay, Nat, are you ready?" Hinata asked her, her kind eyes glimmering through her hipster haircut bangs.

"One second, Hin." Paul interjected. "We need to talk with our girl." Nat and Jackie nodded and the three formed a tight circle.

"Natalia, we know you love Maddy," he said.

"Aaaand, we know she loves you. I mean, I saw her out there. She looks positively melancholy," Jackie added.

"So, you're going to go out there, and pour out your heart, right? I mean, that's what you do. It's why your fans love you, and why we love you. Get your girl back, Chambers."

With that, he pulled both women into a bear hug and kissed Nat on the cheek. She took a deep breath, fought back some tears, grabbed her guitar and nodded to Hinata, who climbed the stairs to the stage and took the mic.

"Good evening, Brooklyn!" Hinata growled into the mic, getting the crowd amped up. Nat caught a glimpse of Maddy's red hair, but Maddy had yet to spot her.

"I know tonight is Open Mic Night," Hinata continued, "but we are going to kick off the evening with a special performance from an old friend of Icon and one of New York's finest singer songwriters. Give it up for Nat Chambers!"

The crowd whooped and hollered, sending up whistles and cheers, which filled the space and practically carried Nat on to the stage with a wave of love. When she got to the stage, she found herself making direct eye contact with Maddy, who stood slack-jawed and frozen in place. Nat hated seeing her like that.

"Hey everyone, I'm so glad to see you all and be back at Icon tonight." Maddy's eyes now flashed at her, and she grabbed her purse.

"The reason I'm crashing your open mic is because I'm in love."

She swallowed hard as the crowd let out murmurs of, "Aw," and shouts of "Yeah!"

Maddy stopped where she was.

"So I met the most incredible woman. I mean, you guys, she sparkles. And, I'm going to be honest. I fucked it up. I didn't mean to but that's not the point. That's never the point is it, when the person you love is hurting?" She looked down at the stage floor. "I have spent the last month kicking my own ass because I may have screwed up the best thing that ever happened to me. And through all that kicking, and a fair share of drinking, I wrote something. I hope you don't mind if I play it for you tonight."

She ran her fingers across the strings as the audience cheered. When she looked up she was terrified that Maddy would be gone, but she was still there, clutching her purse but standing firmly in place. With that, Nat strummed the opening chords of her song.

I'll stand up, or shut up, or crawl to your door
There's nothing or no one that I've wanted more.
Wherever you go, whatever you do, I'm in, Madeline.
You can scream, you can swear, I'm still standing right here.
Keep me at arm's length or drown me with tears,
Whatever you say, whenever you land, I'm in, Madeline.
If your heart has a space, if there's still a small place, for me, for you.
Let me wipe it all clean, let me re-write this scene,
Just say no, or hello, or come on back in, Madeline.

As Nat looked at Maddy, she could see tears welling in her eyes. Her face had softened, and now she looked at Nat with not a hard mask of anger, but something hopeful. Nat's voice soared through the empty spaces of the bar, cutting through the hot air given off by the bodies swaying before her.

I would wash it away, I would reset the day.
I will give you my heart, would you take it I pray?
Wherever you go, whatever you do, I'm in, Madeline.

As the final chord rang out, the crowd's applause broke through the stillness. Across the bar, a smile slowly formed on Maddy's lips and her heart leapt. She handed her guitar to one of the guys in the front of the audience and hopped off the stage into the crowd. They parted and she closed the distance between her and Maddy, until they were standing right in front of each other.

"I'm sorry," she whispered. "I am totally, crazily, utterly in love with you."

Maddy took a deep breath of relief and let out a small laugh. She raised her hands to Nat's cheek. "I let my insecurity get the best of me. I have missed you so much, Natalia."

From within the crowd, Nat could hear a voice cry out in a decidedly British accent, "Kiss her already, you wanker!" *Thank you, Jackie.*

And that's exactly what she did. She leaned in and kissed Maddy, slowly and softly, which brought forth a deafening cheer from the audience. It was a performance no one would forget anytime soon.

When they finally broke the kiss, she stepped back to take Maddy in. "Do you want to go somewhere and talk?"

"Yes, let's go to your place," Maddy responded, lacing her fingers through Nat's. Nat looked around for her friends and could see Hinata, Jackie, and Paul, all standing near the stage, giving her looks of approval and thumbs up. Paul had Nat's guitar now, slung over his shoulder. He motioned for her to leave.

They didn't say much as they hailed a cab and slid into the backseat. They held each other's hands tightly, sending glances each other's way as the driver yelled at bike messengers and complained about the surge of traffic these days. When they arrived at Nat's apartment, Eddie ran to Maddy, who scooped him up and peppered him with kisses. She placed him, still purring madly, on the couch and turned to Nat.

"When I saw you with Melissa, it was like all these old feelings rushed in. Rejection, fear, all the things I've been pushing down inside of me for so long. "

Nat ran a hand through her own hair. "It makes me sick to know that you felt that way. I never, ever meant to hurt you."

"I know you didn't."

"I had no idea that Melissa was going to be there. When she kissed me, I was more shocked than anything. I didn't want her. I don't want her. You shouldn't have had to see that, and I will forever be sorry."

Maddy closed the space between them and wordlessly pulled Nat's shirt over her head. Nat did the same in return, kissing Maddy hard and fast as they undid each other's belts, buttons, and zippers. There would be no time to make it to the bedroom, and Eddie yelped in disapproval and ran off as they tumbled onto the couch. Nat worshipped Maddy's breasts as she murmured and moaned beneath her. She moved down Maddy's torso, kissing every freckle she could find, until she was between her legs, tasting her. How could someone be so delicious? Her tongue made wide sweeps of Maddy's sex. Like sugared pears and the ocean, so sweet and heady. She slipped a finger inside as she focused her attention on Maddy's clit, causing Maddy to practically buck off the couch. She dug her hands into Nat's hair and cried out. Nat made her way back up, nibbling and caressing Maddy's breasts as Maddy's chest heaved, trying to recover from her orgasm.

"Don't ever stop touching me like that," Maddy said breathlessly, as a wicked smile crept across her lips.

"I promise," Nat said as she slid in beside Maddy on the couch. They faced each other, and their mouths were drawn together like an unstoppable force, something otherwordly and singular in its desire. Maddy slid her hand down the length of Nat's naked body, between Nat's legs mirroring the way their tongues slipped between each other's lips.

"I've missed this," Nat said as Maddy's fingers plunged deep within her.

Maddy lowered her head and her mouth joined her fingers in delighting Nat. "And I've missed the way you taste." Maddy's tongue flickered faster and faster until Nat could barely keep her body on the couch anymore. When she came, she saw stars. Nat wasn't done yet, though. She quickly caught her breath and pulled Maddy into her arms. They switched places and Nat held Maddy from behind, rocking her girlfriend onto her knees. Nat used one hand to rub Maddy's already swollen clit, and the other to tease her tender breasts. Maddy's ass ground into Nat's thighs as she kissed and sucked Maddy's neck. Maddy's orgasm came again hard and quick, and Nat clutched her as Maddy went limp in her arms. Then they laid together, in a sweaty exhausted heap, kissing and whispering words of love until they drifted off to sleep.

Maddy's sleeping and naked form was illuminated by strips of light that seeped through the blinds of Nat's bedroom windows. Nat propped herself up on an elbow and looked at her girlfriend, whose breathing was still heavy with slumber. Eddie, too, was fast asleep, tucked up next to Maddy's knees, his fat paws outstretched.

It had been three days since their reunion and they'd barely left the bed. Maddy called in "lovesick" to work, which is apparently a thing you can do when you are a hotshot pastry chef. Nat had successfully dodged Oliver's calls and only responded to the giddy and teasing texts from Paul and Jackie. She and Maddy had lived on little sleep, delivery food, and each other. While it was pure bliss, Nat knew she couldn't hold off much longer on Oliver, and Maddy wasn't going to win a James Beard Award making pancakes in her underwear in Nat's kitchen. When Maddy stirred, Nat traced a finger along her smooth forearm. A smile rose to her lips, her eyes still closed.

"Kiss me," she whispered, in a voice caught halfway between awake and sleep. Nat obliged, starting at her silky neck and working down her back, feeling goose bumps rise beneath

Nat's lips. When she reached Maddy's toes, she kissed each one separately, wishing them good morning, which made Maddy laugh.

"Come back here," Maddy said, and Nat threw herself down beside her, causing Eddie to murmur his disapproval for being ruffled.

Maddy pulled her in for a kiss, the smoky taste of sleep still on their lips.

Nat wrapped an arm around her waist. "Baby?"

"Mmm?"

"We have to re-enter the society of the living soon."

Maddy scrunched up her face and said, "Pfft," with her tender lips and finally opened her eyes. "But I like it so much better in your warm bed," she purred, which sent a tingle through Nat's spine and between her legs.

"I know," she said as she gently pulled Maddy on top of her. "But we have jobs and friends, and there's brunch out there in the world." She eased Maddy onto her knees and slipped between her legs. "Some with bottomless mimosas." With that she pulled Maddy down onto her face and wrapped her hands around Maddy's bottom.

Between moans, Maddy said, "Why would I...oohhhh... want bottomless mimosas...oh god...when I can have this?" She soon came against Nat's talented tongue. "Okay, we can have brunch. But after I work up an appetite," Maddy declared as she worked her way down Nat's body with a fever, eager to return the favor.

CHAPTER THIRTY-TWO

Nat and Maddy were cuddling in bed when Nat's phone buzzed with a message from Paul, who was apparently on the same wavelength.

Brunch? I want you to meet Ryder. Jackie's coming too.

This brought a smile to Nat's face. This was serious. Meeting the friends. She couldn't remember the last time Paul introduced them to one of his gentlemen friends.

"You have the most amazing smile," Maddy said as she gazed at Nat. "What's the good news?"

"Well, I think Paul wants us to meet his…boyfriend."

Maddy cocked her head. "Paul has a boyfriend?"

"Yeah, I know. I was surprised too. I think he's in love."

"Wow, well then we most definitely have to meet them. When and where?"

Nat quickly sent a text and got one back with a time and place. "In an hour, at Fly the Coop on the Upper West Side."

"Well then, we'd better hurry," Maddy replied.

Nat looked her gorgeous girlfriend up and down and bit her bottom lip gently. "If we're going to make it in time, we should probably shower together."

Maddy tossed her head back and laughed. "Yes, what a sensible, time-saving measure."

Nat stripped off the covers and chased Maddy into the bathroom.

Nat and Maddy arrived at Fly the Coop fifteen minutes late, fingers entwined and freshly scrubbed. Paul stood up and motioned them to a table where Ryder, Jackie, and surprisingly, Steve, waited.

"Well, well, well," Nat murmured to Maddy. "Looks like Paul's not the only one who has found herself a boy."

She shot a look at Jackie who just smiled and shrugged her shoulders like, "I know, right?"

They made their rounds, hugging and kissing cheeks. Nat gave Steve a quick jab to the ribs, and his handlebar mustache twitched in a smile. When she got to Ryder, a handsome dark-haired man with a five o'clock shadow, he put out his hand for a shake. She looked at it and made a "tsk" sound as she pulled him in for a tight hug. He soon relaxed against her and returned the embrace in earnest.

They all took their seats, Paul with his arm slung around Ryder's chair, Steve and Jackie leaning into each other, and Nat and Maddy with their hands on each other's knees. When their round of mimosas came, Nat raised a glass and the others followed.

"To this ragtag group finding a little bit of heaven."

"Here, here," Paul added.

"*Prost!*" Jackie declared.

They settled in to chatting and Nat was quickly enchanted by Ryder's easy sense of humor and infectious laugh. It didn't hurt that Paul was wickedly funny and took joy in making his boyfriend lose it whenever he could. Jackie shared the tale of sneaking into her first music club and seeing a rock show, and how it transformed the way she thought about music. Steve did impressions of his bandmates, which were scarily accurate.

As Maddy talked freely and sweetly about her adventures in France, Nat watched with loving eyes. She loved hearing the tinkling sound of her voice, and her loud, quick laugh when she was really tickled by something.

"Chambers." Paul's voice sliced into Nat's dreamlike state.

"Yeah?"

"Have you spoken to Oliver yet?"

She thought back to looking at her phone and the missed calls from her manager.

"I have not."

Paul cut into his chicken and waffles. "Well, he says it's important, and I quote, 'to get your head out of your pants and call him asap.'"

She blushed. She could see Maddy and Jackie were lost in conversation, so she excused herself to make a call.

Oliver picked up on the first ring. "Jesus Nat, I've been trying to reach you for days."

"Sorry Oliver, I've been…"

"Oh, I know what you've been doing. I'm happy for you. Thrilled. It's actually one of the reasons I've been trying to get ahold of you."

"Okay, so what's up?" she asked, her interest piqued. Normally Oliver didn't show the slightest interest in her romantic life.

"Did you know someone filmed your performance at Icon?"

The thought hadn't really occurred to her, but then again, people were always whipping out their phones at live shows, so it didn't exactly surprise her. "No, but does that really matter?"

"The video has gone viral. The song, your kiss with Maddy. Someone uploaded it to YouTube and it's got…300,000 plays so far! You are a listicle on BuzzFeed. 'The Top Ten Crushworthy Songs by Nat Chambers.' My phone has been going nonstop. That was some seriously romantic shit, Nat."

"So…this is a good thing?"

"Are you kidding me? I'm fucking salivating over here. This is like a manager's dream."

She was taken aback, but glad that others were getting something out of all of this, but she hoped Maddy wouldn't be upset about it. It's one thing to date someone in the public eye and another thing altogether to be thrust into the public eye yourself.

"I'm sure you won't be surprised to hear that I got an earful from Melissa Hartford's manager, but I told him to take his tour and shove it right up his ass. We never needed them, and we sure as hell don't now, considering I have a stack of requests and potential tour dates waiting for you to take a look at. I even got a request for you and Maddy to be the special guests at a Pride Parade in Montana in a couple weeks!"

Montana. That was where Maddy had grown up and the place she fled all those years ago.

"Long story short," Oliver said, "We have a lot to talk about. Come by my office tomorrow, if you can pull yourself away from looooove."

"Okay. I'll see you then."

She hung up, her head filled with so much more than she expected the call to contain. She walked back into the restaurant, its walls and ceiling pinging with the sound of happy voices and conversation. Maddy was leaning over her plate, engrossed in what Ryder was saying, while Steve and Jackie stole a kiss. When she sat down, Maddy nuzzled her ear and pulled away.

"Is everything okay, baby?" Maddy asked.

"Yeah. Yeah, I think so. We, uh, we apparently have a lot to talk about."

CHAPTER THIRTY-THREE

Maddy paced the floor of Nat's living room as Nat sat on the couch and watched her parse through the information that was recently dumped into her lap. Nat's stomach roiled, a nervous feeling settling in as she waited for Maddy to speak.

"So, everyone in the world knows about us?" Maddy asked as Eddie followed her, rubbing his gray face against her shins.

Nat cringed. In all this time, they had been so busy falling in love and then being apart, they had never discussed what it would mean once their relationship was really out in the open. "It appears that way," she replied, an unexpected softness in her voice that made her feel small.

It stopped Maddy in her tracks. She walked over to Nat and knelt beside her, taking Nat's hands in her own. "Nat, I love you. I thought I lost you and now we're here. Nothing changes that. Sure, I didn't expect our anonymity as a couple to vanish overnight, but if that's the price I have to pay to wake up next to you every morning, it's worth it."

A smile crept across Nat's face. "You want to wake up next to me every morning?"

Maddy let out an exasperated sigh. "Yes, I do. But we can talk about that another time."

"When," she asked, her voice hopeful.

"Natalia."

"Okay, okay, so what do we do now? I mean, what do you want to do now?"

Maddy bit her lower lip. "I don't know yet, but I think you should take me to bed."

Wordlessly, Nat kissed her softly and Maddy crawled into her lap. She buried her face in Nat's neck and bit down softly on her shoulder as Nat's hands slipped under her shirt.

Later, after moving to the bed and recovering from their bliss, Nat remained hovering over Maddy, their naked limbs burning and entangled. She nipped at Maddy's chin. "So?"

"So? Natalia Chambers, are you trying to charm me into talking so soon after you made me orgasm because you know I'm as weak as a kitten for you?"

"Maybe," she said as she shifted her thigh, brushing against Maddy's already stimulated sex.

Maddy hissed through her teeth. "Fine, talk, just don't stop doing that."

"Montana. You haven't been back in a long time."

Maddy arched her hips against Nat. "That's true."

"I can have Oliver tell them no thank you. Send them our best wishes, but that we have a scheduling conflict."

Maddy reached her arms around Nat and pulled her close and tight. Nat could see in her eyes that she was once again close to pleasure, her pupils huge and dark in the glow of the lights of Queens. Maddy shivered in her arms, letting out a soft cry of satisfaction. Nat covered her mouth with a kiss, Maddy's tongue cool and sweet. Maddy pulled away from the kiss, gazing into Nat's eyes.

"No. Tell them we'll be there, and we'd be honored."

"Really?" She sat up, not believing her ears.

Maddy propped herself up on her elbows. "It's not every day you get asked to be the special guests at a Pride Parade. Besides, I'm proud to be yours. I don't care if Instagram or anyone else knows. In fact, I've just decided I want them to. At first, it was a little intimidating, I admit. But I've never felt this way, and I want to shout it from the mountaintops." Maddy wriggled her naked body out from underneath Nat and jumped on the bed, lifting her hands to her mouth like a bull horn. "I. Love. This. Woman," she mock shouted.

Nat laughed wildly and tackled her back onto the bed. "And I love this woman," Nat whispered before she smothered her in kisses.

CHAPTER THIRTY-FOUR

As the plane approached Missoula, Nat could hardly believe her eyes. She gazed out the window at majestic mountains and waterways winding through the lush greenery. She turned to tell Maddy, but she was sweetly sleeping, her head brushing against Nat's shoulder. Knowing that the stunning creature sitting next to her grew up nearby, breathing in the crisp clean air, running barefoot through the grass in Kalispell, made Nat smile. She may have run away from her old life and her father, but Maddy spoke fondly of her childhood, picking mint and splashing around in Flathead River. An idyllic time before the reality of adulthood and intolerance set in. Nat gently leaned closer to the window to catch a view of snow-capped mountains in the distance.

"That's Glacier National Park," a croaky voice announced next to her. Maddy was bleary-eyed but smiling. "You look like a goofy little kid."

"In all my travels, I just missed it, you know? I guess I pay special attention to beautiful things now. Kiss me."

Maddy shook her head and covered her mouth. "No, I have nap breath."

"My favorite kind. Come on, I need to kiss you over the mountains."

Maddy leaned in and obliged.

A staticky voice buzzed in from the cockpit. "Hello there, ladies and gentlemen. We are beginning our descent into Missoula, Montana, home of some of the best trout fishing in the US."

"Oh, thank god," murmured Nat. "You know I've been dying to get my trout on."

"You'd look good in those waders with nothing on underneath."

"Now you're talking." Nat laced her fingers in Maddy's until they safely landed. Maddy lifted her feet off the ground during landing, and it was remarkably endearing. After debarking, they walked hand in hand through the small airport and found a driver holding the Miss Chambers and Miss LaDuke sign.

"Freaking fancy," Maddy whispered as they followed the driver outside to the car.

"I know, right? We're like bona fide celezbrities here. There's just the right amount of flannel in this state, and I feel so safe and welcomed."

"It's also kind of confusing, trust me," Maddy added. "Is she a lumberjack, or is she a lesbian? Is she both? My teen years were fraught and filled with a lot of plaid-laden fantasies."

"Huh," Nat replied. "I learn something new about you every day."

"We'll pick you up a nice Montana flannel and we can have some fun times when we get home. Me with a bottle of red, you in a flannel and nothing else."

Nat let out a delighted sigh. "Good heavens, woman! I might just pass out."

"It's the altitude. You'll get used to it."

It was a short ride to the bed-and-breakfast, a stunning Victorian home, with charming owners and even more charming grounds.

"So pleased to have you here, Miss Chambers and Miss LaDuke," said Rebekah, one of the owners. "We're huge fans of *Trauma University*, and our son has all your albums, so we borrowed some of them in anticipation of your arrival."

"Well that's great to hear," Nat replied, turning on the charm. "I'd be happy to sign one of them for him if you think he'd like it."

"Absolutely," she said, clapping her hands together with delight. "You must be tuckered out. Let's get you settled into your room. We have set up some sweets and champagne on the balcony for you. I hope you like the pastries, Miss LaDuke. My husband is an amateur baker but he loves it."

Maddy flashed Rebekah a huge, genuine smile. "I'm sure I will, and I can't wait to try them."

This was something Nat loved about Maddy. She was always so kind and gracious to everyone. Nat could be aloof sometimes, standoffish, but Maddy was always warm and made everyone feel at ease.

Rebekah opened the door for them. "This is our finest suite, and we hope you feel at home here. If you need anything, just let me or my husband, Jeff, know."

With that, she took her leave and left Nat and Maddy alone. The room was grand, in the way Victorian rooms often were, with a four-poster bed and clean white linen sheets. The antiques were in mint condition and gave the room an authentic feel. A fireplace stood in the corner, and she secretly hoped for a chill in the air that night so they could cuddle up next to the inviting fire.

Maddy wrapped her arms around Nat's waist and placed a soft kiss on the back of her neck. "Welcome to Montana, baby."

"Welcome back, Maddy. Are you okay?"

She breathed out against Nat's neck. "I think so. I have you by my side. I thought I would feel...I don't know...anxious? But, instead I feel at peace."

Nat faced her and tucked a loose strand of ginger hair behind her ear. "I'm so glad to hear that."

"You know what else I'm feeling?"

"Hmm?" Nat cocked an eyebrow.

"Starving. Can we go to dinner now?"

She smiled and pulled her phone from her back pocket. "It's only three."

Maddy took her phone and tossed it on the bed. "My stomach is on New York time."

Nat's own stomach growled in agreement. "Damn woman, you are always right." Her gaze scanned the room and landed on the small bistro table set up outside with champagne and pastries. She nodded in the table's direction.

"Why not?" shrugged Maddy. She opened the windows, letting in a sweet, cool breeze. Maddy picked up a pastry that looked like a cross between a scone and a muffin. She bit down and looked shocked, causing Nat to laugh out loud.

"What's wrong?"

She winced and grabbed a glass of champagne. "I think he mixed up the sugar and salt. Now you really need to take me out to dinner."

Nat grabbed her hand and they ran out of the room and flew down the stairs. On the way, they caught sight of a middle-aged man straightening up the parlor, his shirt dusted with flour.

"You must be Jeff," Maddy called to him. He nodded heartily. "Lovely pastries, thank you so much."

Nat could barely contain her giggle, but Maddy was doing a kindness, and Jeff blushed and stammered out, "thank you."

They headed toward downtown Missoula.

"That was awfully nice of you," Nat commented as she took Maddy's hand.

"A person can learn how to bake. He'll get better because he loves it. He was probably nervous, and we've all mixed up our ingredients at one point or another. You should have seen my first attempts at filo dough. *Une catastrophe.*"

"I love when you speak French."

"Oh yeah," purred Maddy, slowing her stroll and taking Nat by the waist. She leaned in but Maddy pulled away cheekily. "How about, *je vais t'embrasser, après on mange.*"

Nat licked her lips and rubbed her nose against Maddy's. "And what does that mean?"

"It means…" Maddy brushed her lips against Nat's, sending a shiver of desire up Nat's spine. "…I'll kiss you after you feed me."

CHAPTER THIRTY-FIVE

After dinner and with bellies full of chicken-fried steak, they decided to take a stroll. The streets of Missoula's downtown were already prepared for the following day's Pride festivities. Rainbow flags hung from lampposts while businesses showed their support with placards and posters in the window. Queer couples were out and about, doing the same thing as Nat and Maddy, eating great local food and enjoying the perfect night air. A few yards ahead of them, a gay couple kissed in front of an ice cream shop. Maddy's hand slipped through Nat's and held it tightly.

"This is unreal to me," Maddy commented as they walked past groups of people at sidewalk tables dining and laughing.

"How so?"

"I didn't know this world existed so close to my own as a young person," she said, her voice quiet and thoughtful. "I wonder what kind of a difference it might have made to me back then."

"Maybe you would have run off to Missoula and not Paris?" Nat teased.

"Well, let's not get ahead of ourselves," she replied with a smile, "although this town is pretty great. I have vague memories of visiting when I was a kid, but it certainly didn't involve this," she said, pointing at a rainbow flag gently flapping in the breeze.

"Are you excited about tomorrow?" Nat asked as they rounded the corner and headed into the more residential area back toward their bed-and-breakfast.

"Yes, and also a little nervous," Maddy replied. "I've been to pride in Paris and New York, but always as a spectator, never a participant."

"Same," Nat said. "I'm usually stuck behind a gaggle of gays or a cadre of drag queens. I have a feeling this is a little more low-key."

Maddy squeezed her hand. "Oh, you think?"

"I mean, I certainly hope there are cadres of drag queens. A girl can wish. We'll have to wait and see."

CHAPTER THIRTY-SIX

You couldn't have asked for a better September day for a parade. The sky was a deep blue and the temperature was in the low seventies. It allowed for stunning views of the vistas in every direction. Rainbow flags were out in force and crowds lined up to celebrate the LGBTQ community.

Nat had decided to go with the Montana flannel motif and wore a cleanly cut-off flannel shirt, a collar chain, black jeans and boots. Maddy was more in the spirit of Pride, donning a "Love is Love" shirt, jean shorts, and rainbow knee socks. Nat was beside herself when Maddy had come out of the bathroom that morning.

"What?" Maddy asked, taking stock of her own outfit when she saw the look on Nat's face.

"It's…It's just so…adorable. You are like the cutest thing I've ever seen."

Maddy blushed. "Well, when in Rome—or Missoula. And you look like the kind of lumberjane I only dreamt of when I was a baby gay."

After getting picked up by an Uber, they arrived at check in and were greeted by two excited Pride organizers.

"Hello Nat and Maddy!" a frazzled but smiling older woman said as she reached out her hand. "I'm Cheryl Blackburn, the president of the pride organization. I can't tell you how excited we are that you were able to make it, and on such short notice."

"We're thrilled to be here, Cheryl. Thank you for inviting us," Maddy said as she shook the woman's hand.

"Maddy, having a Montana girl like you making it big means a lot to us here. I think a lot of the young folks look up to you."

Maddy placed her hand on her heart. "You have no idea what that means to me."

"And Nat, everyone here are huge fans of your music, and of course, *Trauma University*," Cheryl said. "Are the rumors true? Are they going to add a lesbian character this season?"

Nat grinned. "Cheryl, your guess is as good as mine, but I really hope they do."

"Well, let's get you two ready for the roll out." Cheryl motioned to a young man with a Montana Pride shirt and a clipboard. Erik, can you escort Miss Chambers and Miss LaDuke to the car they will be parading in?"

"Certainly, Cheryl. Ladies, follow me," Erik said as he made his way through the crowd of volunteers. He led them to a plum-colored 1957 Chevy convertible. "You'll be sitting here." Erik patted the backseat of the mint-condition car.

"Wow," Nat said. "This car is ridiculously cool."

"Not too shabby, is it?" Erik said. "One of our donors is a classic car collector and he loans out his collection for Pride. Honestly, this is the best car here. I'll be your driver too. Just sit back and relax. We'll be starting soon. Would you like some cold water, tea, anything like that?"

"Water would be great," Maddy said and Erik went off in search of the beverage.

Maddy sat on the side of the convertible and slid her legs into the car. "This backseat is huge. I bet a lot of teenagers got up to no good here over the years."

Nat hopped in after her. "We could always ask Erik to close the top so we could test it out."

"That would really make an impression on Missoula, wouldn't it?"

"We would blow. Their. Minds," Nat said, her eyes widening.

Erik returned with their waters and they broke out into giggles. "Okay, it's time. Are you ready to go?"

"Yes!" they said in unison.

The engine roared to life and Erik honked the horn at some passing volunteers who offered thumbs-up and waves in response. "I'd tell you to buckle up, but we'll be going three miles an hour so I think you'll be okay. Feel free to sit on the back of the seat too if you want to have a better view." They did as he suggested and hopped up.

They chugged down a side street, the noise from the crowd getting louder and louder as they approached. When they turned down Main Street, the street was three people deep. It was hardly the size of a New York or San Francisco Pride, but the crowd was filled with excited, smiling faces. As the Chevy passed, Nat and Maddy saw signs that said things like, "We Love You Nat and Maddy!" and "ChamberDuke Are Relationship Goals."

Maddy turned to Nat. "ChamberDuke?"

Nat chuckled. "I guess that's our portmanteau."

"We have a portmanteau? That's…so…weird and also amazing."

The parade route wasn't incredibly long, but Nat thought it was exhilarating. Seeing so many happy faces and people celebrating who they are was what Pride was all about. In New York, Pride was an institution, a party with sponsors and professional floats. Here in Montana it was obvious the floats were handmade and local businesses donated to the cause. Seeing peoples' hard work in action gave her a new perspective.

Before they knew it, Erik had turned down another side street and the parade was winding down. "Thanks so much, you two," he said. "Now we have the festival and we have a spot for the two of you to meet some eager Montanans."

"Sounds good to me," Nat said as she swung out of the backseat and offered her hand to Maddy. Maddy climbed out and into her arms for a big hug and kiss.

The organizers set them up at a table where they could sign autographs and talk with members of the community. The table was covered in rainbow confetti that kept getting stuck to her arms, but Nat didn't care. She got to meet a lot of smiling faces, some shy, but always kind. She couldn't seem to wipe the smile off her own face, especially when Maddy attracted fangirls of her own.

"Um, I'm like, literally obsessed with your Instagram, Chef Maddy," said a young curvy woman with bright eyes and dyed purple hair. She clutched the hand of an equally excited women with short curly hair and an undercut that was growing out.

Maddy beamed. "That's amazing, and you can just call me Maddy."

"Um, okay, Maddy. I've been like, super inspired by you and I enrolled in the culinary program at Missoula College for next year."

Maddy stood and opened her arms to the young woman, who rushed into them.

"I'm so proud of you. I know you will make an extraordinary chef one day." The young woman burst into happy tears, and it was all Nat could do not to follow suit.

"By the way," the young woman said, with wet tear tracks cutting through her foundation, "I made your Love Muffin recipe for this one," she said as she motioned to the woman beside her.

Maddy grinned, turning to the young butch. "And? What did you think?"

"Well, I asked her to marry me before I was even done with the first one."

"School first, then marriage?" she asked, and the women nodded. "Good call." She opened her arms again for a group hug.

As they walked away, hand in hand, Nat leaned over to her and whispered in her ear. "You. Are. Spectacular."

Maddy returned the compliment with a kiss. More people came up for chats and autographs, and soon the festival was clearing out and the line trickled down to a few.

A handsome older man with a gray and ginger beard walked up to the table as Nat and Maddy scribbled away at autographs, but he turned away at the last moment.

"Hey, don't be shy! Thanks for coming," Nat exclaimed, waving him over.

It wasn't until she saw the ashen look on Maddy's face that she knew something was amiss.

He took a deep breath and looked straight at Maddy. "Hello, Madeline."

She stiffened. "Hello, Dad."

CHAPTER THIRTY-SEVEN

Nat didn't know it was possible for the air to be sucked out of the outside, but that's exactly what happened as she witnessed Maddy lay eyes on her father for the first time in seven years. She touched Maddy's hand and found it trembling beneath hers. Maddy's father looked visibly uncomfortable as he shifted on his feet before them.

"Uh, do you think we could…that we could speak alone for a moment, Madeline?" he asked.

"No," Maddy quickly replied. "Whatever you have to say, you can say it in front of Nat. My girlfriend. How did you know where to find me?" Her voice quaked as she tried to push out the words and Nat felt helpless to ease her pain.

He cleared his throat. "I have a Google alert set for you."

She narrowed her eyes. "What?"

"I, uh, I've been following your career for years now. When I saw the video, and then the announcement that you would be here…I guess I couldn't find a reason not to try and see you."

"Oh, I can think of a million, Dad." She spat out the last word like a dagger, and it seemed to hit her father like a blow.

"Listen, I can see this is a bad time. It was a mistake to approach you here, but I'd really like to talk to you. There's a lot I want to say, and I just haven't had the guts until now. I'm staying here at the Payne Inn. I'll be there until tomorrow night, if you would like to talk. I hope to see you, Maddy." With that, he nodded at Nat, tucked his hands into his pockets and walked away.

Maddy fought her tears and squeezed Nat's hand tighter. When he was finally out of sight, she crumbled into Nat, who ushered her away to a quiet spot where they could be alone. Maddy let out a sob against Nat's chest, and Nat just held her until the crying subsided.

She finally raised her tear-stained face. "Why? Why would he come here and ambush me like that?"

"Oh baby, I don't know. Maybe he realized how much he's been missing out on?" Nat kissed her on the forehead and eyelids. "Sometimes people change."

She let out a bitter laugh. "Well, sometimes it's just too late. I managed to survive the last few years without him or his approval, and I don't need it now."

Nat suspected she wasn't being honest, but decided it was best to keep that thought to herself.

"My head's killing me. I need to go back to the inn and take a nap," she said wearily.

"Let me get our stuff."

Maddy shook her head. "No, you stay here. There are still fans who want to see you. It's a celebration. Plus, I could use the alone time right now, baby." Maddy kissed her gently on the lips. "I'm going to walk, okay?"

Nat nodded and watched her walk away like a wounded deer. She knew she had to do something. She pulled out her phone and typed Payne Inn into the search box.

CHAPTER THIRTY-EIGHT

The Payne Inn was one of those moderately priced hotels where traveling businessmen and women stayed and got drunk from the mini bar while watching CNN in the comfort of their own rooms. When Nat walked in, the place was quiet except for the faux jazz Muzak that floated from the ceiling's built-in sound system.

The agent at the front desk was entertaining herself with a round of Candy Crush. "Hi, this is kind of a weird question but I'm looking for someone. Well, a guest. His last name is LaDuke... He has graying red hair and a beard...mid-fifties?"

The agent smiled her best hospitality smile and said, "I believe the man you are looking for is currently sitting at the bar." She pointed to a sad looking wood bar with a too-small TV playing ESPN over it, and a red-haired man sitting with slumped shoulders.

She thanked her, walked over to Maddy's father, and quietly sat down beside him. "It's club soda," he grumbled, swirling his straw around the glass. "I gave up drinking a few years back but sitting at a bar still calms me somehow."

She nodded.

"I just didn't want you thinking that I was some kind of old drunk," he continued, not yet looking at her.

Her face flushed as she sat there, and the realization that this was a terrible idea washed over her. But here she was. "I'm Nat Chambers. I'm Maddy's...errr..."

"I know who you are," Mr. LaDuke said, cutting her off.

Well at least that was out of the way. After a moment of silence, he shifted on his stool and looked her in the eye for the first time. He had the same eyes as Maddy, not quite green, not quiet brown. Perfectly hazel.

"I saw the video of you two at the rock club. The one everyone is making a fuss over."

Suddenly she felt very shy. "Oh."

He took a sip of his soda. "Maddy looked happy. She looked happy today too. I'm really grateful for that. So, I guess I should thank you."

"You don't have to thank me, Mr. LaDuke. Maddy's the best thing that's ever happened to me."

"Aiden," he grumbled.

"Excuse me?"

"You can call me Aiden. Let's do away with the formalities, shall we?"

She nodded in agreement.

"So, Nat, why are you here instead of my daughter? Did she send you to tell me to get lost?"

She shook her head. "No, I came on my own. I really don't know why."

He laughed a hard, little chuckle. "Well, at least we're starting off on an honest foot."

She bit the inside of her cheek. "The better question, Aiden, is why are you here?"

"At the Payne Inn? For the competitive rates and the make-your-own waffles of course," he said with a smirk. Now Nat understood where Maddy got her dry sense of humor.

"The truth is, Nat, it's been a long time since I've seen my child. I miss her. I miss her more than you could ever imagine."

She swallowed a lump that formed in her throat.

"I've done a lot of things wrong in my life. Wasn't the best husband. Put my pride before my family. I hurt my daughter in ways that I am still grappling with." He motioned to the bartender to refill his glass. "I can't tell you how many times I've wanted to talk to her. To hear her voice on the other end of the line. But each time I decided to reach out, the shame of what I had done and the reasons why she ran... Well, they did a number on me. I simply wasn't brave enough. Then when I saw you singing your heart out in that video, and the love and joy that filled her face...I decided that being a coward was no longer an option. I owed it to myself and Maddy to be brave."

Nat felt he was telling her his deepest truth. He had lost a daughter and he wanted a chance to get her back one day.

"What's your plan then, Aiden?"

He took another long sip of his soda. "Well, I think that's entirely up to Madeline now. It may have been seven years, but if I know one thing about my daughter, it's that she needs to be in control of her own destiny, with or without me."

The bluntness of his statement felt like a kick in the gut, but she knew he was right. If there was ever to be a real reunion, it would have to come from Maddy. He was in stasis until then, something he had long ago accepted. She also knew she had to get back to Maddy right away.

"Aiden, I'm glad to have met you, and I hope we can do it again sometime." She stood and held her hand out to him. He took it and shook it firmly.

"I hope so too, Nat."

CHAPTER THIRTY-NINE

When Nat returned to the bed-and-breakfast, Maddy was sitting on the small veranda watching dusk settle across the property. She walked out to the veranda and sat beside her.

"When I was a kid, summer felt like this. It even smells the same," Maddy said. "Sitting here, I can almost hear my mother's voice calling me inside. It's been nearly twenty years since she died, and I had forgotten what she sounded like. Being here triggered a memory, I guess."

"I'm guessing something else probably triggered it too," Nat suggested, testing the waters.

Maddy sighed deeply. "Yes, Natalia, you are probably right about that."

They sat in silence as a family of deer ran through the yard below, the little ones kicking their legs and jumping along their way.

"How was the rest of the event?" Maddy asked.

"I don't really know. I left right after you did." Maddy shot her a puzzled look. She licked her lips and prepared herself for blowback. "I actually went to see your dad."

Maddy didn't say a word at first, simply blinking at her in disbelief. Then she stood and walked into the room. Nat joined her, ready for whatever was in store, which was more painful than what Nat was expecting. Tears welled in her eyes.

"What gave you the right to do that, Natalia?" she asked softly, her cheeks red and wet with tears. "He is *my* father. There is a reason for all of this. I thought you understood that."

Nat nodded, trying not to cry herself. "I don't know why, Maddy. I guess I just wanted to see if his intentions were true. I didn't want anyone to hurt you again, especially the person who was the cause of so much pain for you."

"That's not your goddamn job, Nat. You are my girlfriend, not my bodyguard."

Maddy was right. She had overstepped in a big way. "Baby, I'm so sorry. It wasn't my place. I took away your autonomy and that was fucked up. Please forgive me." She took Maddy's hand and kissed it. She didn't pull away, and instead she sat down heavily on the bed, and Nat followed her lead.

Maddy wiped away tears, her cheeks soggy now. "Well. What did he say?"

She was surprised but was quick to answer. "He's never forgiven himself for pushing you away…and he misses you. He said he was so glad to see that you were happy now. I guess he wanted to know he hadn't broken your spirit along with your heart."

"I… I can't think about this now. Besides, we have a plane to catch in the morning." Maddy pulled her clothes off the hangers in the closet and shoved them into her waiting suitcase. Nat did her best just to stay out of the way of the flying garments and went down to the lobby to give Maddy her space. She tried to occupy herself with some of the dusty books in the library, trying to tamp down the dread that she'd made another huge mistake with Maddy. When she came back in, Maddy was already in bed, clutching the covers. Nat climbed in next to her, and when Maddy's body relaxed at her gentle touch, Nat held her tight until they fell asleep. Nat dreamed of the deer that night, the doe following the others in the gloaming.

The sound of the blow dryer woke Nat up, and she could see Maddy dressed in a towel through the open bathroom door. She'd never seen Maddy actually dry her hair, so she knew she meant business.

When Maddy reappeared in the bedroom, she locked eyes with the sleepy Nat. Maddy took a deep breath.

"All this time, I've been protecting myself, but I've been changing and growing too. It never occurred to me that he might have changed too. I never let myself believe it. Nat, I need to see my dad today."

She kissed Maddy's cheek and pressed her forehead to hers. "Whatever you need. Whatever you want. I'm here for you. Are you still mad at me?"

"Oh hell, yes," Maddy said, her eyes wet but dilated. "Come here." They hugged each other tightly. "Reschedule the flight?"

Nat nodded. "I'll have Oliver take care of it. I'm sure we can stay another night here at the inn, too."

Maddy returned to the bathroom to get ready and Nat quietly slipped out of bed and got dressed. When Maddy returned, she looked pleased that Nat was buttoning up her shirt and wearing skinny black jeans and boots.

"I wasn't sure if you wanted me to be with you today. I figured I'd get dressed anyway," she explained, securing the top button of her shirt.

Maddy ran her hands through Nat's hair, down her neck, and over her collar. "I wasn't sure either until right now, but now I can't imagine doing this without you by my side."

She took Maddy's hands and kissed her fingertips. "I love you, Madeline. I am here and I always will be."

"I know, baby. I love you too," Maddy whispered. "Now go finish getting ready, I have an estranged father to visit."

CHAPTER FORTY

"Can you please ring Aiden LaDuke?" Maddy asked politely at the front desk of the Payne Inn.

A few minutes later her father exited the elevator, smoothing his thinning hair with a quick brush of his hand. Now that the two were in the same room again, Nat could see just how much Maddy favored her father. Of course, the hair and the eyes were similar, but she also had his full lips and square chin.

Maddy and her father awkwardly greeted each other with a brief hug. He motioned for them to take a seat on one of the leather couches in the lobby. Nat and Maddy sat on one, while he sat opposite them, his hands on his knees.

"I want to thank you for coming here today, Maddy. I know these circumstances aren't ideal."

She simply nodded and took Nat's hand, squeezing it tightly. He clearly noticed the gesture between the women.

"That Nat's a hell of a girl. She's got cojones the size of Oklahoma. I hope you didn't give her too much hell about coming to see me."

Nat opened her mouth to speak but thought better of it when Maddy gave her hand another squeeze.

"So, why are you here, Dad?" she asked, her face stern but not entirely unyielding.

He rubbed his palms on his khakis. "I came here to say I'm sorry. I know that doesn't feel like enough. I know it isn't enough. But that's what I am. Sorry. A sorry man who has lost too many years with the daughter he loves. Maddy, when your mother died, I lost myself. She was the love of my life and I have never been the same. But that's not an excuse for being a mean sonofabitch who smacked his kid when he found out she was gay."

Maddy shivered at this, and Nat could feel it through their held hands.

He continued. "What I did…was terrible. I've done a lot of soul searching. I talked to preachers, to therapists, to God, but mostly, I talked to you. I know you can't hear me, but I talk to you all the time and I ask your forgiveness."

She didn't skip a beat. "It's been seven years, Dad. Why now?"

He nodded like he knew that this was coming. "Well, I've wanted to talk so many times, but honestly, I was afraid you'd slam the door in my face. I joined PFLAG two years ago—"

"Really?" Maddy and Nat asked in unison.

This made him chuckle. "Yes, in fact, I'm the current treasurer for our chapter."

Maddy sat back, a look of surprise on her face.

"If I hadn't had their support, I wouldn't be here today. I also met my lady friend, Susan, at the group. She has a gay son, and she's always waving rainbow banners and marching in parades. I think you'd like her."

"Susan sounds like a badass," Nat exclaimed, and for the first time in the meeting, Maddy's face broke into a smile.

"She's very special," he said softly. "I'm a lucky man. She's taught me a lot."

"Wow," Maddy declared. "The tough as nails Aiden LaDuke actually learned something…from a lady?" There was a hint of bitterness in her tone, but she softened it with a half-smile.

"I've changed a lot, Madeline, but I don't expect you to just accept that at face value. I would like the opportunity to show you. Would you be willing to talk on the phone sometime? Whenever it's convenient for you? I have a real cell phone now. Susan made me trade in my flip phone. I even text."

"Whoa, texting, let's not get ahead of ourselves," Maddy said. He glanced at the floor in disappointment, but she said, "Yes. We could try a phone call sometime."

This made him grin, and for the first time, Nat could see the dimples that hid beneath his beard. He took out a piece of scrap paper from his pocket and scribbled his number down, handing it to her. She stood as she took it and tucked it into her purse.

"Your birthday is next month. Maybe I can call you then."

"You remembered."

"Of course, I do." She tugged on Nat's hand. "We should be going. We have that lunch meeting."

He stood as well and stuck his hand out to Nat, pulling her in for a hug. "I know she wouldn't be here if you hadn't stuck your neck out," he whispered. "Thank you."

"This was all Maddy," she replied, giving credit where it was due.

This time Maddy approached her father for a hug, and gone was the earlier awkwardness. They headed out, but Maddy stopped before they hit the exit.

"Dad!" she called.

He turned to look at her.

"I'm glad you came."

CHAPTER FORTY-ONE

Nat and Maddy lay in bed, Maddy's head resting on Nat's shoulder. They hadn't spoken much since they'd returned to the inn, but they'd made love softly but urgently.

"Hey," Nat whispered. "Are you okay?"

Maddy shifted, her hair gently tickling Nat's arm. "I think so." Her hands traced their way down Nat's stomach. "It's so dark out here. In the city there's so much ambient light, you never see the stars. I used to sit for hours as a kid and look up at the heavens. Now I can't remember the last time I even saw a constellation."

Nat sat up in bed. "Then let's do it. Let's go see the stars. There's a huge backyard out there, just waiting for us."

"Really?" Maddy sat up too.

"Yeah." She got out of bed and wrapped a sheet around herself. "Come on. Show me Orion."

Maddy giggled. "Natalia, you're naked."

"Um, I'm wearing a sheet. Hurry, grab the comforter. We'll slip down the stairs. Everyone is asleep."

"You're nuts," Maddy said as she wrapped the comforter around herself. "And I guess I am too."

They snuck out the door, opening it slowly so it wouldn't creak. They padded down the stairs while the world slept and slipped through the living room and out the side doors leading to the great lawn. Nat giggled quietly as they ran through the soft grass to a clearing that seemed to reach to the end of the universe.

Nat let her sheet fall to the ground and Maddy followed suit. They laid together, their heads touching, as they gazed upward.

Maddy pointed. "Now that's Orion. He's always pretty easy to spot. Just look for the belt. And that is Ursa Major. And close by is Ursa Minor."

"Talk about your sibling rivalries. I think Big Ursa is my favorite. Where'd you learn all these?"

"My dad if you can believe it," Maddy said quietly. Neither spoke for a moment, but then Maddy broke the silence. "I'm going to call him."

Nat leaned in and kissed her naked shoulder. Maddy practically glowed under the light of the moon, like she herself was a heavenly body. "Are you cold?"

"A little. Come here, baby, and warm me up."

Nat cuddled closer and draped the sheet over her.

"I love you so much, Natalia."

"I love you so much, too."

"Oh Natalia, look!" Maddy pointed to the right of their view. "It's a shooting star."

"Get out, I've never actually seen one," Nat said, her heart aflutter.

They watched the star blaze across the sky, a last hurrah before disintegrating into the earth's atmosphere. She reached for Maddy's hand and they held each other close as the star disappeared from sight.

CHAPTER FORTY-TWO

The next morning Nat woke up and Maddy's side of the bed was cool to the touch. She looked around and saw that Maddy wasn't in the bathroom or the balcony. She grabbed her phone and her robe and cracked open the door to their room. Downstairs she could hear the low bass of a man's voice and Maddy's tinkling laughter. She crept down the stairs into the kitchen. Maddy stood there in jeans and a white T-shirt, a flowered apron wrapped around her waist. Her hair tumbled around her face as she giggled and instructed Jeff, the innkeeper.

"You don't want to overmix. That's really the key. Your dough will end up tough if you keep jostling those gluten molecules around. Doesn't matter if it's puff pastry or pancake batter."

He beamed as he mixed a bowl of dough. "Got it, Chef. I think I've been man-handling my gluten."

Maddy noticed Nat in the doorway and shone a bright smile in her direction. "Hi, baby. We're making *Chassons aux poires* for breakfast."

Nat got such a thrill when Maddy said things in French. "I have no idea what that is, but it sounds A-mazing."

"It's pear pastry," Jeff announced proudly. "We're just getting the first of pears and Chef Maddy suggested we go with the bounty of the Montana season."

"I bet she did," Nat said, winking at her girlfriend.

"Okay, Jeff, that should be good to rest for a bit. You'll want to slice these pears about a quarter of an inch thick. And please, call me Maddy."

He nodded. "You got it, Maddy."

Maddy led Nat down the hallway. "Morning, baby," she said as she wrapped her warm hands around Nat's waist and kissed her neck. "Mmm, you smell like sleep. All soft and nutmeg-y."

"It's really sweet of you to cook with Jeff. I bet he's totally fangirling," Nat said, her nose nuzzling Maddy's cheek.

"Some days you just have to bake, baby."

Nat brushed a tangle of red curls out of her eyes. "Did you sleep okay?"

"I guess the fresh air last night did something because I woke up this morning feeling amazing."

"Or, you know, something else could be helping with that too," Nat suggested.

Maddy looked into her eyes and nodded. "Yeah, that could have something to do with it, too."

"Hey," Nat said, motioning for Maddy to sit on a divan in the hallway. "There's something I've been meaning to show you." Nat pulled out her phone and flipped through pictures until she landed on the one Paul had taken in Paris. She showed the phone to her.

Maddy gasped and raised her hand to her mouth. "Oh my god, that's Carm's. And you! And a *baguette*!"

She nodded. "When we played Paris, I knew I had to find it. I wanted to see where you found your spirit. I guess, it helped me find mine again too. Monsieur Bouchard gives some hella good advice."

Her eyes widened and glazed with happy tears. "Phillipe. You spoke to Phillipe?"

"Yeah, I saw your picture at the shop. You look like such a kid."

"I was."

"I wanted to understand where you came from. I wasn't sure if I'd ever see you again, but when I stepped into that shop, I felt you everywhere. It was amazing. Also, I am prone to grand, often disastrous gestures." She ran her fingers across Maddy's soft cheek.

Maddy caught her fingers and kissed the tips. "This I know."

"Phillipe sends his love, by the way."

She clasped her hands against her heart, turned her head and sniffed the air. "Do you smell something burning? How is something burning? We're not even at that stage yet."

"Uh, Chef, I mean Maddy," Jeff's voice called. "I think I need your assistance."

"You. Are. Crazy. And I adore you," she said softly, before running back into the kitchen.

CHAPTER FORTY-THREE

When Nat and Maddy returned home, life was a whirlwind. Nat and the band knew they would be a go soon for studio-time, so the remaining weeks were filled with lots of rehearsals and trying out new songs at local shows. Nat was quickly becoming the queer music it-girl and while it was exciting, it was also a little intimidating.

Maddy was also becoming the girl with the golden crust. It was amazing what a viral video could do for a person's popularity. Touché was booked solid for months, and the critic from the *Daily Press* returned and gave Maddy that elusive extra star. Also, her Instagram was smoking. Maddy and Nat would take selfies and share with their followers, who seemed to adore the singer and the chef as a couple. A picture they snapped of having coffee in bed together got more than 50,000 likes and not only were they now navigating a serious relationship, they were doing so as a couple in the public eye. While Nat would get anxious, it was Maddy who always managed to bring her down to earth.

"I can't imagine what it would have meant to me to see a picture of a couple like us when I was a teenager," Maddy said one night in bed after a particularly exhausting day of rehearsals, baking, and interviews. She was wearing Nat's Dolly T-shirt, a true sign that Nat was head over heels in love.

"Yeah," Nat said, putting her arm around Maddy and tracing the line of her hips. "You're right. What we're doing matters."

"Mmm, keep doing that. My hips are killing me today. I forgot my Crocs and wore my Converse instead. Now I have marble glaze on my Chucks and a sore hip."

Nat applied more pressure with her thumb and index finger, making Maddy moan in relief.

"So… What are you doing for Christmas this year?" Nat asked, knowing her question was out of the blue, but she'd been thinking about it for weeks.

A smile crawled across Maddy's face. "I usually work but Touché is closed this year. You're asking me about Christmas when it's barely October?"

Nat leaned up and kissed the exposed skin of her hip. "Yeah, I know. How about spending Christmas with me and my family? Please?"

Maddy chewed thoughtfully on her lip. "It's been a long time since I really celebrated Christmas."

Nat nodded.

"Like your *family* family?"

"Yeah, my mom has been relentless about it. She wants to meet the woman I can't stop talking about."

"Well," Maddy cocked an eyebrow, "I mean, who wouldn't, right?"

"She follows you on Instagram."

Maddy blushed deeply. "She does? You didn't tell me that."

Nat shrugged. "She doesn't use her real name. I think her username is BraziltoBuffalo or something like that."

Maddy lifted her fingers to her lips. "I'm extremely mortified and also flattered."

She pulled Maddy closer and spoke, punctuating her words with kisses. "Spend. Christmas. With. Me."

Maddy let out a small whimper when she kissed her right under her ear. "Ask me again."

This time Nat lifted herself up and kissed Maddy on the lips. "Spend. Christmas. With. Me."

She licked her lips and ran her fingers down Nat's face.

"Paul, Jackie, and Ryder will be there too."

"No Steve?"

"Redfern will be in Europe so expect lots of those weird firecracker tube things and paper crowns. What do you say?"

"Yes. You had me at paper crowns," Maddy said as she pulled the covers over both their heads.

CHAPTER FORTY-FOUR

"Raz Chadha?" Nat yelled into the phone as she stood in the rehearsal studio with Jackie and Paul. "Hold on Oliver, I need to put you on speaker. Okay, you have all three of us now."

"Okay, gang, I have some killer news. Raz Chadha is going to record your new album," Oliver said, as Jackie and Paul hugged.

Raz Chadha, was one of the most sought-after recording engineers in New York and a huge step up from the band's last producer.

"This is incredible, Oliver," Nat shouted into the speaker phone. "When is this happening?"

"Raz has a surprise opening in his schedule at the beginning of December, so we're going to shoot to record then. I know it's not a lot of time—"

"It's fine. We've been practicing the new songs since we got back. We'll be ready. Tell Raz, we can't wait to work with him."

"Will do. I'm assuming you'll be recording in his personal studio in Midtown, so Paul…no vaping please."

"Fine, fine," Paul said with a grimace.

"And Nat, stay healthy. We don't have time for one of your bouts of laryngitis. Wear a scarf or take some shit, okay?"

"Yes, I'll take so much vitamin C that my pee will be fluorescent," she said and nodded.

"And Jackie?"

"Yes, Ollie?"

"You're perfect. I have nothing to bitch at you about. Okay, I'm going to let you all go now and get back to practicing. Talk to you all soon."

Nat ended the call and looked at Paul and Jackie. "Raz freaking Chadha."

Jackie's eyes were big. "Didn't he produce…"

"Yes," Nat cut her off.

"And…"

"Yes!"

"This is most exciting. Paul, aren't you excited, love?" Jackie asked.

"Yes, of course. He's also bi and super cute," Paul said. "I've seen him at the Teddybear leather parties."

"Since when are you into the leather scene?" Nat asked.

He rolled his eyes. "I go where the wind takes me, Natalia."

"Okay, so, moving on," Nat said. "Let's go home and cuddle up with our respective significant others and drink lots of green smoothies because we're going to be pretty much living at the studio soon. We know what we're doing with these songs now, and I don't want to drain the life out of them before we get to work."

When Nat got home, she wasn't surprised to find Maddy working on a new recipe. She swooped in and kissed her on the cheek.

"Babe, that smells amazing. What is it?"

Maddy wiped her hands on her apron. "Well, I'm working on a gluten-free cinnamon roll recipe that doesn't taste like disappointment."

"What's the verdict so far?"

"The first three batches are currently residing in the dumpster, but this one… Well, I have hope for this one. Want to try?"

"Um, of course."

Maddy plated a hot cinnamon roll and handed it to her with a fork. She took a bite and Maddy was right. She had nailed it with these. "You'd never know these were gluten-free," Nat said through a mouthful of cinnamon goodness.

"Terrific. Now that I know what to do right, I can play around with them and deconstruct them. Thanks, babe. It's so nice to have an official taster in the house."

She took a small bow. "Hey, I have awesome news. Raz Chadha is going to be our producer for the album! He's a big shot and he's worked with some of the best acts on the East Coast."

"Oh that's wonderful news! I'm so excited. When do you start?"

"Soon," Nat said as she undid the knot in Maddy's apron. "Which means I need to get as much of my Maddy on as possible now."

"I'm yours," she said as Nat dipped her and kissed her slowly.

"Mmm, wanna dance?" Maddy asked.

It had become their little thing.

"You know it," she replied as she grabbed the stereo remote and put on some music.

She took Maddy by the hand and led her to the living room. Eddie rubbed against their legs as they danced together in the middle of the day.

"I didn't go to prom," Maddy said as they swayed to the music.

"You didn't?"

"No, at the time I thought it was dumb. Now I realize it was because I didn't think I could dance with a girl."

"I went with a friend who tried to stick his tongue in my mouth all night," Nat spun Maddy out, then back in. "I finally left him at the dance to go to an afterparty with a particularly curious cheerleader."

"Of course you did," Maddy said, squeezing her tighter. "Do you think you'll need tasty provisions in the studio?"

"That would be amazing. What have I done in this world to deserve you?" she asked, playfully, but with truth behind the question.

"Must have been the same thing I did to deserve you."

CHAPTER FORTY-FIVE

Raz Chadha rubbed his chin stubble while adjusting a number of knobs and levers on the soundboard. Nat, Jackie, and Paul watched nervously from behind their glass partitions, their headphones on and instruments in hand. He lifted a finger, then hit the intercom.

"That's a wrap. That's it, folks. This album is going to be hot shit," he said, his voice coming in hot over their headphones.

"Are you serious?" Nat asked over the com.

"As serious as a heart attack."

She sighed with exhaustion and joy as Paul and Jackie burst out of their rooms to join her and hug it out in hers. Raz motioned for them to join him in the main booth. He held out his hand for high fives but ended up getting pulled in for a hug himself.

The trio plopped down on the leather couch behind him as he swiveled his chair around to face them. "Seriously, I'm not blowing smoke up your asses. This is fantastic. Obviously I need to work my magic." He cracked his knuckles and added, "But you laid a hell of a record down."

"Raz, thank you, man. There's no one we would rather have had on this journey with us. You've been amazing. What do the logistics look like?" Nat asked.

He sucked his teeth. "Honestly, the stuff I have to do is pretty minimal. I'm thinking a completion right after the new year. Then you're probably looking at a late spring release with the label."

"Kick. Ass," Paul said as he took a drag on his vape. What Oliver couldn't see, wouldn't hurt him. "Does this mean I can go on vacation with Ryder? I've been wanting to take him away for a week, but I'm always with these two beardless babes."

"You don't know my life," Jackie quipped back.

Raz chuckled. "Yeah, dude, your vocals are good and your drums are always spot on. I don't need you. What do you think, Nat?"

"I think you're an angel from heaven. After Christmas, Paul, enjoy the world with your man. We're taking a break from touring for the winter. I know we can all use a little R&R."

Jackie lit up. "I think this means I can surprise Steve in Oslo or wherever the hell he is for New Year's."

"Absolutely. I'm going to try and spend as much time as I can with my beautiful girlfriend...and writing," Nat said.

"Jesus, just a few months ago you couldn't write a word, now you're the goddamn lesbian Victor Hugo," Paul said.

"*Lez Miserables*...with an emphasis on the lez. But also happy," Jackie added.

"Thank you, Raz," Nat said, reaching out her hand.

He shook it and then stood. "All right, time for you unreasonably good-looking people to get out of here and let me work my magic." He made a shooing gesture with his hands, and the trio grabbed their gear and headed out the door.

"I can't believe it's done!" Jackie exclaimed as they walked down the chilly Lower East Side street together. The air was dry and cold but the city was full of life and holiday lights. "I love this album so much, Nat. It really is the tits."

"None of this would be possible without you two. I know we're the Nat Chambers Band, but without you, this doesn't exist," she said, linking her arms through Jackie's and Paul's.

"God, you are so gay and sappy, Chambers," Paul said. "But thank you."

"Oh yeah, something else. I've discussed it with Oliver and he told me I could tell you personally," she said with a smile. "From now on, we are splitting the profits of everything, from merch to tour sales, an even three ways."

Jackie and Paul stopped in their tracks and stared at her. Just then the first snowfall of season began falling.

"Holy shit, you aren't just making it rain. You made it snow!" Paul exclaimed.

"Seriously, I was never in this for the money, but I'd be foolish to say that I don't realize how money can change things for people. I know it did for me. Oliver says with this album, new licensing deals and spring tour, we're on track to make at least triple what we have in the past."

"Well, Merry bloody Christmas to us all," Jackie said.

CHAPTER FORTY-SIX

It was indeed a white Christmas that year and Nat's loft twinkled with soft lights hung from a large tree she and Paul bought on the corner of Astoria Boulevard and Thirty-Fourth Street. Nat loved that particular tree stand because the sellers were two delightful young women from Montreal who brought in the sweetest smelling trees. They had to lug the tree for a dozen blocks, but she knew it would be worth it. Paul griped the whole way, but when he saw it all lit up and smelled the pine in the air, she swore she saw a tear glisten in his eye.

Nat's parents had arrived the day before Christmas Eve and were staying at the boutique hotel down the street. Nat offered them her spare room but her mom declined, not wanting to "cramp her style."

But now her mom fluttered about the kitchen, checking on the turkey and rice with raisins, a tradition from Nat's Brazilian grandmother. Her father sat quietly in the living room as Eddie purred away on his lap, listening to Ryder talking about the mystery he'd always wanted to read starring a trans detective leading character. Paul and Jackie were debating what went better in eggnog: rum or brandy. Nat's mother chimed in with a suggestion of cachaça.

Nat's stomach growled at the smell of the food cooking, but also tossed and turned knowing that Maddy would be there soon. She had never brought a girl home for the holidays, and while she wasn't technically bringing Maddy home, this was still the first time she'd be meeting her parents. Maybe it was the whimsy of the decorations or the sweet sounds of Christmas music floating through the room, but her heart was already soaring. She was in one hell of a Christmas spirit.

The buzzer rang and she ran to the door to let Maddy up. Maddy gently rapped at the door, and she swung it open and greeted her with a huge smile.

"Merry Christmas, baby," Maddy said, wearing a sweet red dress that was parent appropriate but still enough to jingle Nat's bells.

"Merry Christmas," she said as she leaned against the doorway. "You have a key, you know."

Maddy reached out and tugged at her festive sweater. "I know, but I wanted to make a good impression. Don't want your parents thinking we're living in sin." She whispered the last word.

"Oh baby, they totally know. My mom didn't want to interrupt our 'unwrapping of presents,' so they're staying at that new little hotel down the street."

She licked her lips. "Mmm, I love them already."

She led Maddy in and was met with cheers from the other guests. Nat's mother ran over to Maddy and swept her up in a huge hug.

"Finally!"

"Merry Christmas, Mrs. Chambers," Maddy said sweetly, handing her a bottle of wine.

"Oh, no, no, no. You must call me Valentia!"

"Can I call you Valentia?" asked Nat.

"Show some respect, *filha*," Valentia said with a cheeky grin. "Now, come, take off your coat. Look at how gorgeous you are. Natalia, don't screw this up. I want to keep her."

Maddy shot a wink at Nat as Valentia whisked her away.

"Your mom was right. This nog really works with the cachaça." Ryder lifted his cup. He had an eggnog mustache, which somehow he pulled off.

"If I've learned anything, Ryder, it's that Valentia is always right. Or at least, that makes my life easier," piped in Nat's dad, Brian. He now had his own cup of nog, and he and Ryder raised their glasses together.

"I'm thinking perhaps we shouldn't have whipped out the nog until after dinner," Nat said as Jackie placed a paper crown on her head.

"What's the fun in that?" Jackie said.

Valentia and Maddy took up residence in the kitchen after introductions were made to Nat's dad, and they were all giggles like they had been best friends for years.

Nat leaned over the island. "You know, Mom, Maddy works in a kitchen every day. Maybe she should have tonight off?"

Maddy shook her head. "Are you kidding? Your mom is going to teach me her *brigadeiro* recipe. Can you believe I've never made them?"

"Natalia, mind your business. The chef and I are bonding, and I'm going to share my extra special recipe with her." She turned to Maddy and said, "I used to make these for Nat when the other girls would pick on her in junior high."

Nat blushed. "Well, thanks mom for ruining my cool street cred."

Maddy laughed as she tied an apron around her waist. "So you mean to tell me that Nat wasn't always a super-cool rock goddess?"

Valentia waved her hands. "Please, they used to call her Ratty Chambers."

Nat sighed. "You snitch on someone smoking in the bathroom one time... I think I'm going to go over there and die now. Thanks and happy holidays." She walked over to her bandmates and poured herself a cup of nog.

"So, when do you leave for Oslo?" Nat asked Jackie.

"On the twenty-eighth! Steve was so excited. We're going to see some fjords and do a little Viking roleplay."

"Well that sounds exactly right. And you and Ryder? What's the plan?"

Paul sipped his nog. "Well we're going to the Keys for a week. I rented us a little beach house. You know what he's most excited about? Seeing those six-toed cats. Isn't that right, Ry?"

"Hemingway's cats are legendary," Ryder chimed in as he joined his boyfriend at the nog station. "Besides, life's about more than tea dances. Sometimes you need to stop and smell the key lime pie, honeybear."

"Ryder, have I told you lately how much I like you?" Nat asked.

"Well you told me when I arrived, then when the crudité platter came out, and now. So, yes. And thank you." He squeezed Paul's hand.

"Hey sweetie, why don't you and the gang play a few Christmas tunes while your mother and Maddy finish up?" Brian asked.

The trio looked at each other and shrugged. They had played some Christmas shows the year before, so it wouldn't be that hard to come up with a few tunes. Nat picked up her guitar while Paul grabbed a small handheld drum and Jackie settled in beside them. They sang "White Christmas," "O Holy Night," and "The Christmas Song," while the aromas and sounds of the holiday filled the air. She would sometimes catch Maddy's eye in the kitchen and feel warm and tingly all over, like she'd just had a cup of mulled wine. When they were finished, Brian and Ryder clapped and hooted.

The sounds of a clinking glass rose above the noise. Valentia stood with a glass and a fork in her hand, calling everyone to attention. "Okay, folks. Dinner is ready! Natalia, open the champagne."

After the party had stuffed themselves silly on the feast, and of course, a slice of Maddy's Figgy Pudding Cheesecake, everyone settled into comfy chairs and couches to chitchat and drink coffee. Maddy sat with her knees slung over Nat's lap, as everyone debated what was the greatest Christmas album of all time – The Carpenters *Christmas Portrait* or *A Jolly Christmas* from Frank Sinatra.

Maddy excused herself and stepped out onto the balcony with her phone in hand. Nat could see her through the glass door, the light of the phone illuminating a small smile on her face. After a few minutes, she put down the phone and looked out at the falling snow and twinkling city lights. Nat grabbed a throw and joined her outside, wrapping her in the warm blanket.

"Looking for Santa?" Nat asked, sliding her arm around Maddy's waist. "I don't think he gets to the East Coast until after midnight."

Maddy chuckled softly and leaned into her hug. "Is that so?"

She nodded. "Did you remember to ask Santa for what you wanted this year?"

Maddy turned and looked at her, snowflakes settling into her hair and fluttering across the bridge of her nose.

"I already have everything I want, baby."

She leaned in and kissed Maddy's chilly lips, their cold noses rubbing against each other.

"I called my dad just now."

"How'd it go?"

"Actually, pretty well. He was excited to hear from me. I could hear people in the background, and he put Susan on the phone to say hello. She seems really nice, and he seems happy. It was good. Each time we talk, it gets...easier?"

She nodded. "And you're okay?"

Maddy looked out onto the shimmering city below. "Yeah, Nat. I'm more than okay. I'm really good." She turned and smiled, and Nat's heart melted in spite of the snow and cold.

They headed back inside and Nat's parents were the first to call it a night. After hugs and kisses, they left for their hotel with promises of returning the next night. Paul and Ryder stretched and yawned, exposing their fuzzy bellies full to the brim. Jackie downed her glass of wine and complained about needing to pack for her trip to Europe, although it was clear she was over the moon happy to be heading to see Steve. There was a group hug before the three departed, and finally Nat and Maddy were alone to change into their Christmas jammies, which were discarded on the bedroom floor not long afterward.

CHAPTER FORTY-SEVEN

Nat could never stay in bed on Christmas morning. She slipped on some comfy pants and a tank top, then headed to the kitchen to make some hot cocoa and whipped cream. When she returned to the bedroom, Maddy was spooning Eddie, her bare shoulder kissed by the winter sun. Eddie opened one green eye, yawned and stretched before promptly falling back asleep. Nat set the hot cocoa on the nightstand and crawled under the sheets beside Maddy.

"Mmm, you're so warm," Maddy murmured. "Wait? When did you put on clothes?"

"Merry Christmas. Don't you want to see what Santa brought?" Nat asked with the impish grin of a child.

"Yes. Gimme one second."

"Eddie, it's Christmas," Nat said.

Eddie chirped but did not share Nat's enthusiasm. A few minutes later Maddy padded into the living room, smelling like a candy cane, and plopped herself into Nat's lap. She kissed her neck, which helped shake the remaining sleep off.

"It looks like there's a present under the tree for you," Nat said and motioned to a medium-size box wrapped in colorful paper and ribbons.

"Wait, me first," Maddy interjected. "You have to unwrap your present from me first."

"Okay, where is it?" she asked, trying to hide her excitement.

Maddy sat up on her knees and motioned to her shirt, which was buttoned all the way up.

"You're my present?" she asked, her face flushing.

"Well, not exactly," Maddy motioned for Nat to unbutton her top. Nat slowly undid Maddy's top button. "Keep going." Nat undid the next button, revealing more of that creamy skin that drove her wild. When she got to the third and fourth button, resting between Maddy's breasts, a necklace revealed itself. Nat took the warm metal and ran it between her fingers. On the front was an image of Ursa Major, with diamonds as the stars. On the back was written, "The night I knew I was forever yours."

Nat choked back tears as she held the pendant in her hands. Maddy reached around her neck and unhooked the necklace and fastened it around Nat's neck.

"I love it, thank you," Nat said finally.

Maddy ran her hands through Nat's hair. "Good, I'm glad. I have more for you."

"No!" Nat replied. "My turn!" She reached under the tree and pulled out the box and slid it over to Maddy, who tugged at the strings and paper. When she opened the box, she burst out laughing.

"Crocs! You got me a pair of Crocs!" She held up the purple rubber shoe.

"You look so damn sexy in them. But that's not your real gift, silly. Look inside."

Maddy slipped her slender hand into a shoe and pulled out a thin envelope. Inside was a card embossed in gold and made to look like an old-fashioned plane ticket.

"Read it."

"Good for two tickets to anywhere in the world," Maddy read aloud. She squinted at Nat, who was smiling broadly. "I'm sorry?"

"I want to take you wherever you've dreamed of going. You choose when and where."

"Anywhere in the world?" Maddy asked, her eyes wide and excited.

"Yes, anywhere in the world. Rekyvik, Tokyo, Rome, wherever you want."

Maddy tackled Nat to the floor, smothering her with kisses. "I don't know what to say!"

"Say where you want to go and we'll go."

Maddy gazed into her eyes, then kissed her slowly and deeply. "Right now, the only place I want to go is to bed with you."

"That I can do," Nat said just before she got lost in Maddy's eyes.

CHAPTER FORTY-EIGHT

Nat was working on a new song at the studio when a memory flitted into her head. It was like an itch she couldn't scratch, and she knew the only way to soothe it was to do something real about it. She picked up her phone and sent a message to a number that was no longer in her phone, but one she knew by heart.

Hey, it's Nat. Hope you are well. Are you by any chance home for the holidays? A reply came back faster than she anticipated.

Yes, I'm so glad to hear from you.

Nat paused a moment before writing. *Can we meet up for coffee at the old spot? Around one?*

Again, a fast response. *Yes, I'll see you there.*

Nat closed her notebook, grabbed her coat and headed out of the studio.

Nat sat at a banged-up table in a cafe that would be lucky to get a "B" health grade, but she had so many memories trapped in its sticky menus and late night lattes, that she just couldn't stop herself from dropping in from time to time. She tapped her short nails against a hot mug of coffee and watched as steam rose from the one across from her. Coffee with a splash of soy.

When the door jingled, Nat looked up and saw Lara sweep in. She tugged off her coat and sat down across from Nat. Her hair was longer now, which Nat thought suited her.

"I can't believe the health department hasn't shut this place down yet," Lara cracked, which lightened the mood significantly.

"Please, if they did, I'd be out there protesting. I'd be alone, but I'd be there." This made Lara smile.

"Hi, Nat."

"Hey Lara. You look good."

"I am. You look happy."

"I am."

Lara picked up her mug and took a small sip. "I was really surprised to hear from you. Glad, but surprised."

"Well, it's something I've been thinking about for a while and I didn't want another new year to go by without talking, I guess."

"Can…can I start?" Lara asked.

"Go ahead."

Lara blew out a nervous sigh. "For over a year I've been practicing what I would say to you, but now that you're here in front of me, the words feel stuck in my throat."

"Take another sip of coffee. This stuff will loosen up anything." Nat said out of kindness, knowing this wasn't easy for Lara.

"I'm sorry feels worthless. It's not a big enough word to express how I feel. What I did, Nat, was unforgivable. I realize now, with time and some therapy, that I was angry at you."

"Why were you angry at me?"

"Because you had it all. The talent, the confidence, the girlfriend. The band was about you, and I couldn't handle that. So I found a way to sabotage it, I guess."

"In your defense, you had some help from Melissa."

Lara laughed. "It was a supremely fucked-up thing to do, and I have no one to blame but myself. I didn't even really want

Melissa. I was just hurting and I decided she was a way to blow it all up."

"Therapy looks good on you."

"Yeah, it's actually how I met my boyfriend. We met in the waiting room."

"If that isn't kismet, I don't know what is."

"Nat, I truly am sorry."

"I know. Thank you for coming here today and telling me. At the time, I really couldn't hear it. But I can now."

Lara breathed out a small sigh of relief. "Good, because it's my one big regret."

"Really? Because I would think that *Twilight* tattoo you got in Cancun on spring break would have topped the list," Nat said, raising her eyebrows.

"Oh, god. Even after very expensive laser treatments, Edward Cullen still lingers."

"Yeah, he does that."

Lara chuckled. "I have missed the way you make me laugh, Nat. I hope one day we can be something resembling friends again. I know that's a lot to ask, but I want you to know that if you are ever open to that, I'm here."

Nat took a moment before answering. "I'd like that for us too, someday."

"I saw that you have found yourself someone pretty special. I'm so glad, Nat. You really deserve that."

Nat smiled at the thought of Maddy. "Yeah, I got really lucky. Maddy has taught me a lot. I'm so happy for you too. That boyfriend of yours better treat you right."

"Oh, he does," Lara chucked. "He also happens to be a big fan of your music, so you know he has excellent taste."

"Say no more, he sounds perfect."

Lara glanced at her phone. "I wish I could stay longer but I'm heading back to LA today and I have to get to JFK. This meant the world to me, Natalia. You know how to reach me."

"I do." They stood, and for the first time in a long while, Nat opened her arms and welcomed Lara into an embrace. They held each other tight, and the spicy scent of Lara's perfume and her warm hug melted the iceberg that Nat had been dragging around since that night.

"Happy New Year, Nat."

"Happy New Year, La."

CHAPTER FORTY-NINE

Before Nat knew it, the holidays were over and the real world was calling again. Raz had indeed worked his magic on the album and *All In* was even more than she'd hoped. The first time Oliver heard it he cried tears of joy. The trio sat in his office as their manager positively glowed with happiness.

"This is it, you three," he said, pacing, sweat stains appearing under his arms and peeking through his lilac shirt. "Look at me! I'm so excited, I'm sweating."

Paul leaned into Nat. "Well, I guess that's a good sign."

"Are you kidding?" he shouted. "You guys are about to go where you've never gone before. Are you ready?"

Nat, Paul and Jackie looked at each other. "I guess so?" Nat responded.

"Listen, I let a few of the studios hear some of the initial cuts, and well, they're already fighting over your songs. We're talking major licensing, international airplay, and tours playing places bigger than you've ever played before. The label has even given us their blessing to pick an opening band."

"Redfern," the trio shouted in unison before laughing.

"Sure, Redfern, great! God damn, you kids are about to pay off my mortgage."

Nat smiled. "Happy to help."

"You need to keep healthy and get ready. I'll get you a new crew and have them ready to hit the road when the tour begins. This time, though, we make the rules. I don't want you guys getting burnt out. Those days are over. Congratulations! You're hitting the big time."

And as sure as Oliver said it, The Nat Chambers Band became the hottest thing out there. Their song "Take Me There" was all over radio and the Internet and was optioned to be on the soundtrack of a major motion picture. Nat was squeezing avocados in the grocery store when "Do You Wonder at All?" started playing out of the scratchy speaker above her head. The week after that, she was stopped on the street and signed an NYU student's backpack.

And it wasn't just Nat who was noticed. Paul was the toast of the New York gay bar scene, but, happy with Ryder by his side, he mostly just enjoyed the free drinks. Jackie's parents came to visit and wouldn't stop saying how proud they were of their daughter to strangers on the subway. As crazy as life was, coming home to Maddy, who had traded her rental in Manhattan to move in with Nat, was pure bliss. Nat loved it when Maddy slipped into bed after work, smelling like sugar and flour, curling her arms around Nat's waist.

CHAPTER FIFTY

4 months later…

"Dude, you look especially nervous tonight. This isn't our first rodeo," Paul said, slapping his paw on Nat's shoulder.

True, it wasn't their first rodeo, but The Nat Chambers Band was sitting backstage at Radio City Music Hall, and Nat felt a little nervous.

That and she had an engagement ring burning a hole in the pocket of her leather pants.

She hadn't told Paul and Jackie because as much as she loved them, they weren't exactly great with secrets, and she didn't want the big news to slip out over brunch or cocktails. Nat had been secretly searching for an engagement ring for a month, and when she laid eyes on the vintage piece, a large emerald surrounded by fine diamonds, she knew it was the one for Maddy. She was pretty sure Maddy had no idea, and she'd waited until that morning to pick it up from the jeweler to avoid her accidentally stumbling upon it. Now it sat in her pocket, waiting to be united with its intended recipient.

"Nat?" Paul asked, and she realized she'd been in a bit of a daze.

"Yeah, sorry. It's Radio City, my dude. This is like, the dream, right?"

He squeezed her shoulders. "Yup, it is the dream. And Nat, thanks for bringing me along."

She turned to him. "What are you talking about? We wouldn't be here if it wasn't for you. You've talked me off the creating and emotional ledge so many times. I'd still be playing open mics in Brooklyn if you hadn't been by my side."

"But you're the heart, Nat."

"And you're the beat, Paul."

He looked down and had a tear in his eye. "Oh hell, this is gross. Let's never do it again, okay?"

Nat laughed. "Okay, deal. No more sappy, cheeseball emotional business."

"Good. Now I'm going to go warm up, and by warm up I mean smoke in the alley," he said before kissing her on the head and disappearing out the green room door.

Through the speaker, she could hear Redfern wrapping up their set to an excited crowd. Jackie would be watching backstage and would join Nat shortly to get ready for their show.

A quiet knock came at the door as Redfern was greeted with thunderous applause.

"Come in," Nat called.

Maddy slipped through the door, wearing jeans, black boots and a Nat Chambers Band T-shirt that hugged her waist and made Nat weak in the knees.

"Hi baby, are you ready to go?" she asked as she came up behind Nat and slipped her hands down Nat's arms and squeezed her tight.

She swallowed hard. "Not yet. I need to do something first. Can you come with me?"

She nodded, and with a perplexed look on her face, took her waiting hand and followed her out of the green room to a secluded spot backstage. Nat could barely hear the murmuring of the audience above the sound of her own heart pounding. In the spot were a dozen flameless candles. Nat had balked but Radio City Music Hall wasn't about to let her accidently burn the place down just for aesthetics. Still, she had to admit, against the backdrop of black curtains, it looked magical.

"What's this, babe?" Maddy asked, taking it all in.

"My whole life I always felt at home on the stage. It was my safe space, my favorite place, the thing that reminded me that I could dream. When I met you, I found something I never expected to. I found another place to call home."

Maddy's hands began to tremble. "Oh, Natalia."

Nat took her trembling hands and kissed them both. "You are everything I have ever dreamed of. You are every constellation. You are the words to every song. I have never wanted anything more than to spend every day in your arms." She reached into her pocket and knelt down on one knee.

"Oh god," Maddy said, her voice trembling along with her hands.

"Madeline LaDuke, will you join me on life's adventures? Will you do me the honor of becoming my wife?" She realized she too was trembling and could barely catch her breath.

"Natalia. Oh, Natalia." Tears streamed down her face.

Nat cleared her throat. "You're kind of leaving me hanging here, kid."

Maddy laughed through her tears. "Yes! Yes, Nat, I do. I will. I love you!"

Nat felt like she could finally breathe, and she slipped the ring on Maddy's finger. It fit perfectly. She rose and picked Maddy up. They swirled around in an embrace. Maddy grabbed her face and kissed her over and over again.

"God, I love you, Nat," Maddy said, lifting the ring so it could catch the light. She looked around for a moment. "Is anyone coming back here?"

Nat shook her head. "No, I asked to have this space and not be interrupted."

"Good," Maddy said, as she pulled Nat's shirt over her head and pushed her fiancée up against the wall.

"Oh okay, we're doing this?" Nat said as Maddy's tongue caressed the sensitive spot below her ear.

"Hell yeah we're doing this," Maddy said as she removed her own shirt, unbuttoned Nat's pants and slid her warm hand inside. When Maddy's fingers found her sweet spot, Nat gasped with delight. She returned the favor and slid her hand into Maddy's panties, as she kissed and nipped at the tops of Maddy's flushed breasts. It didn't take long before they both came together, kissing each other slowly and intensely.

"I'm going to be your wife," Maddy said softly into her ear.

"Mmm, and I'm going to be your wife," Nat replied, wrapping her hands around Maddy's bare waist. "But first, your future wife needs to play Radio City Music Hall."

"Shit, I almost forgot with all the getting engaged and post-engagement sex," Maddy said, as she reached down to pick up her shirt and button up her pants. She planted one last kiss on Nat's lips. "Okay, I'm going to my seat. I love you. I can't wait to see you out there. Bye!"

Maddy waved as she ran off, and Nat was so full of love and happiness, she could hardly believe it was all real. She quickly pulled herself together and ran back to the green room where Jackie and Paul were waiting.

"What's with you? You're all pink, like a little cherub," Jackie said, rosining up her bow.

"Oh, she's just a nervous Nelly about performing at one of the greatest venues in the world," Paul responded. "You do look a little sweaty, though, now that I'm looking."

She stepped up to the makeup table to blot at her perspiration spots. "Oh, you know, just a case of the jitters."

"Steve said the audience is tits, and we're going to have a blast," Jackie added. "So, take a deep breath and enjoy."

"Yeah, I do feel like I can finally breathe again."

A sharp knock came at the door and a woman in a headset popped her head in. "Nat Chambers Band, this is your ten-minute warning. You have ten minutes."

"Thank you, ten minutes," the trio responded in unison. They gathered in a circle and took each other's hands.

"So, this is it," Paul said.

"Yep, this is Radio City Music Hall. It's absolutely smashing," Jackie said.

"We're going to go out there, and we're going to give them the best show of our lives," Nat added. "I love you guys."

"Love you too," Paul said.

"I love you, pets!" Jackie chimed in. They squeezed each other's hands and jumped up and down together until they were almost breathless.

"See you out there," Paul said as he grabbed a pair of sticks and headed out the door. Jackie picked up her bow, gave Nat a broad smile, and followed after him.

Nat was left alone in the dressing room. She took a long look at herself. Healthy, happy, and ready for the first time in a long time. It was time to hit the stage.

CHAPTER FIFTY-ONE

"Humans and gentle beings," a booming voice called out, hushing the crowd at the music hall. "Radio City Music Hall is proud to present, The Nat Chambers Band!"

The crowd erupted and the sound of their excitement nearly ushered Nat out on stage all by itself. She could see thousands of faces just beyond the blazing stage lights. She lifted her arms in excitement as she headed to her microphone. She slipped on her guitar, tapped her pedals, and lifted her mouth to the microphone to speak.

"Hello, New York. How the hell are you?" The audience screamed in response. "New York is where we call home, and we are honored to be here tonight to rock the shit out of you," Nat said with a devilish grin. Screams and applause followed and the bandmates gave each other a glance. Nat nodded and Paul counted them off with his sticks.

The band launched into one of their older tunes, "Call Her Silver," a song with a driving beat and riffs that made the crowd jump up and sing. Nat wailed away at her guitar and belted the lovelorn lyrics into the mic. Jackie joined her as the melody soared and Silver's story revealed itself, measure by measure.

They played another few tunes, alternating between ballads and up-tempo songs to keep the audience guessing. When they broke out into "Heart/Block" the audience sang so loudly Nat could barely hear herself, and it thrilled her. About a half an hour into their set, she motioned to Paul and Jackie to take a breather. Sweat was forming at her temples and her body hummed with the vibrations of six thousand people.

She took a sip of water and gripped the microphone. "So, a year ago, I got up on a much smaller stage to sing a very special song to a very special person." Some in the crowded whooped and whistled at the mention. "Ah, some of you are familiar," she said, the audience chuckling along. She wiped her forehead. "So yeah, a year ago I asked the most beautiful woman in the world to give me another chance, and she did. And today, I asked her to marry me," Nat said as gasps and screams of excitement filled the room. Jackie and Paul both turned to her with looks of excited surprise on their faces. "And she said yes."

The reaction was deafening, so much so that it seemed to nearly knock her off her feet, but that was actually Jackie and Paul who had run from behind their instruments and tackled her with hugs.

"You asshole!" Paul shouted, as the three of them embraced. "How did you keep that a secret!"

"I'm gobsmacked! Can I be a bridesmaid? No, to hell with that! I'll plan your hen party!" Jackie said as she helped hold Nat on her feet. Nat touched them both gently on the face and they returned to their spots.

As she stepped close to the mic, the crowd had begun to chant, "Madeline. Madeline."

"Yes, that's her name! Maddy, where's Maddy?" She peered past the lights and saw her love with her hand raised in the front row.

"You're crazy," she shouted from her seat.

"You are absolutely right. I am crazy for you." She grabbed her mic, ran down the lip of the stage and hopped into the front row, receiving a kiss from Maddy, which sent the audience into pandemonium.

She spoke into her mic. "That's going to be on YouTube, isn't it?" After stealing another kiss, she returned to the stage. "I mean, it's not every day you get engaged at Radio City Music Hall to the pastry chef of your dreams, now is it?"

She nodded to Paul and Jackie who launched into a beautifully arranged version of "All In," and Nat stood close to the edge of the stage and sang the song directly to Maddy. The crowd lifted their cell phones and thousands of lights lit up the room. When it was over, she blew a kiss to Maddy and one to the audience.

The Nat Chambers Band continued to play the greatest show of their career, which was only just beginning. Everything was just beginning. After the show, Maddy greeted a sweaty and exhilarated Nat backstage with hugs and kisses. Jackie, Paul, Ryder, Steve and the guys of Redfern, and even Nat's parents who had come down to surprise her, all headed over to a local Italian restaurant to drink Negronis and celebrate Nat and Maddy's engagement.

"You sneaky sneak," Jackie said, poking Nat in the ribs. "How did you manage to keep this from us?"

"Yeah seriously," Paul chimed in. "I even know when your period is coming! And you managed to keep a secret proposal from us?"

"What can I say," she replied, wrapping her arm around Maddy's shoulder. "I wanted it to be absolutely perfect."

"And it was," Maddy said and kissed her on the cheek.

"So you lovebirds leave for Japan next Monday?" Jackie asked.

"Yes," Nat said. "That's where Maddy decided she wanted to go. She's obsessed with Japanese pastry and desserts, and I am definitely up for that challenge." She patted her stomach.

"It will be more than just sweets, I swear. I mean, mostly sweets, but still," Maddy interjected.

"You two really are perfect for each other," Paul said, his hand on Ryder's knee. "And trust me, it physically hurts me to say such things. You've really gone and turned me into a mush."

"It's true, and I love it," Ryder replied, before grabbing Paul by the cheeks and kissing him sweetly.

"I don't know about you all, but I'm ready to go to bed," Nat announced. "Getting engaged and then playing Radio City really knocks a girl out."

"Same," Paul replied.

Everyone kissed and said good night, and Nat lead Maddy to a waiting black car.

Inside, Gino called out past the partition. "Hey oh, I heard the good frigging news. Congratulations!"

"Thanks, buddy!" Nat said as she and Maddy slipped into the smooth leather backseat.

"Aw, thank you, Gino," Maddy added.

"Have you set a date?"

Nat laughed. "Well we've only been engaged for like, five hours, so not yet. I'm guessing next year?" Nat looked at Maddy, who was busy wrapping herself tightly around Nat.

Gino nodded. "Where to?"

"Home, please," Nat said. She held Maddy close as they drove down Broadway and onto the parkway.

"Natalia," Maddy said. "I don't want to wait."

"What do you mean, baby?"

She shifted in her seat to face Nat. "I don't want to wait a year to be your wife. Let's get married now."

Nat was taken aback. "Now, as in, *now* now? What about work? What about normal wedding stuff?"

"Yes. As soon as we can. Don't worry about work. We can plan a wedding another time, but I don't want to wait another day to marry you." Her eyes were on fire and Nat could see the passion and love that burned within them. She didn't want to wait either. She nodded her head. "Yes?" Maddy asked.

"Yes, let's do it." She kissed Maddy deeply. "Gino, change of plans. A quick stop at home, and then can you drive us to the airport? JFK?"

"Sure, whatever you need."

Nat let out a big breath and a squeal of happiness. "We're getting married."

"Yes, we are," Maddy replied, running her hands through Nat's hair. "I love you so much, Natalia."

"I love you, too, Madeline."

"Oh, one more thing! We need witnesses." Nat pulled out her phone and shot off a text to Paul and Jackie as the black car sped down the highway.

How do you feel about a little trip to Vegas...tonight?

Bella Books, Inc.

Women. Books. Even Better Together.

P.O. Box 10543
Tallahassee, FL 32302

Phone: 800-729-4992
www.bellabooks.com